Knee Deep

Mac Fortner

Edited by
Daisy Bank Editing

Author Photo by
Ted Trueblood

DEDICATION

*For my wife Cindy, who is always there when I need support and love, and to the **HUNTIN' DOGS** who have been there all my life, and won't go away.*

Life can be as good as you want it to be
The sand, the sun, and the deep blue sea
Just say you'll share it with me
And we'll sail away

Rumora....Mac Fortner

PROLOGUE

Ronnie Pierce opened the throttle on the forty-two-foot Sea Ray and felt the acceleration. He could barely see, even though the moon was bright. The stars twinkled in the sky like a million diamonds. Ronnie wished he had a million diamonds, then he could quit this job, but for now, it paid well and had some interesting benefits. There were times when he could have his way with women before he killed them. Those were the best ones.

He was now at least a mile away from the shore and couldn't see any other boat lights, so he lit his flashlight and shone it around the instrument panel. He located the switch for the lights and turned them on. They did little to show him the way, but at least he could see onboard now.

He turned and looked at the man lying on the deck. His hands were tied behind him, and he had a concrete block roped to his ankle. The man rocked back and forth with the rhythm of the waves. The gag in his mouth prevented him from begging for his life *again*. He had begged – more than most. Usually, they pleaded for about ten minutes and then their voices turned into an unrecognizable babble once they'd accepted their fate.

There was dried blood on his face, but there was a fresh stream now trickling from the corner of his mouth. The gag was becoming saturated.

"You doing okay back there?" he asked his partner, who was guarding the man.

Billie Daryl answered, "Yep."

Billie was a man of few words, but when he spoke, you had better pay attention. He never really spoke words of wisdom, not ones you could ponder the meaning of life from, but words which would unquestionably change your life.

Ronnie kept his eye on the GPS as he opened the boat up a little more.

"This baby can really move," he yelled back over his shoulder.

"You just watch where you're going. If you damage this boat, Juba will have your ass," Billie hollered back.

2

Ronnie kept the throttle down for another ten minutes and then slowly eased it back. According to the GPS, they were right over their favorite spot.

"We're here," he announced.

Billie got up and moved over to the man. "Your ride is over," he said as if he were letting him off a Ferris wheel. "Time to get off."

The man squirmed against his restraints and tried to plead for mercy.

"What? I can't understand you with that gag in your mouth," and Billie laughed.

"Yeah, talk plain English," Ronnie chimed in and giggled like a child. He pulled the gag from the man's mouth.

"Please don't do this. I won't tell anyone," the man pleaded while trying to take in fresh air.

"Sure you will," Ronnie said.

Together they lifted the man from the deck, carried him to the edge of the boat, and set him on the rail. Ronnie held him while Billie held the concrete block so it wouldn't scratch the boat.

"If you had backed off like we told you to, you wouldn't be here now, but oh no, you had to find out what we were going to do with the boat. This is your last ride. Be sure to tell the others down there that we are still doing fine up here," Billie said.

"It wasn't me. It was that detective asking all the questions," the man said, gasping every few words. "I made a deal with you. I only wanted the money. I don't care what you do with the boat."

"Juba doesn't believe you," Ronnie said. "And if we bring you back, he'll have us killed."

"Just drop me off somewhere. You'll never hear from me again," the man pleaded.

"What do you think, Billie Daryl?" Ronnie said.

"Nah."

With that, Billie threw the block over the side, and at the same time, Ronnie pushed the man. They watched him hit the water. He sank instantly, the block pulling him down like the weight on a fishing hook.

Descending into the saltwater, he held his breath as long as he could. He felt the concrete block hit bottom. *Must only be about twenty-five feet here. That was a stupid thought. I should be thinking how to get this block off my leg.* He thought of his wife and his grown children. *How would this affect Terri? Would she still finish her law degree at Notre Dame?* He looked down at the knot securing his leg to the block. With his other foot, he tried to push the rope off over it, but it was too tight. He bent forward, bringing his hands down from behind and fumbled at the knot.

His breath was threatening to release, his lungs burning. He looked to one side and saw the outline of something. In the moonlight cutting through the water, he could now tell what it was—another man, hands tied behind his back. Looking around he saw others. Their eyes were hollow. He gasped at the sight, taking a lung full of saltwater, then everything was gone, and his fear subsided.

~*~

The boat accelerated again and broke plane. Soon it was flying along the water. Just two men out for a nice evening ride.

Teko raised his head, looked over the rail of his fourteen-foot johnboat, and watched the Sea Ray disappear. *What the hell? They just drowned that man. Glad they didn't see me.* "COUNT ME INN— I'll remember that name," he said to himself, reading it on the back of the boat as it sped away.

Teko looked around the moonlit night, wishing his connection would show up before those guys came back. He glanced down at the two hundred pounds of cocaine lying on the bottom of his boat. *I gotta get out of this business before they feed **me** to the fishes.*

KNEE DEEP

Chapter 1

I opened my eyes slowly. I wasn't sure if I wanted to see where I was or what kind of shape I was in. My head was killing me, and my whole body pulsated in pain with every breath I took. I could feel my clothes clinging to my body. I was wet. The sun was fading, but even that hurt my eyes, then I blacked out again.

The next time I opened my eyes, it was dark. At least I hoped it was because I sure as hell couldn't see any light. The pain was still there. Maybe even some new pain that I didn't feel the last time I'd woke up.

I felt my right arm which was where most of the pain seemed to come from. I didn't feel any bones sticking out. That was a good sign, but I thought I had clothes on the last time I checked. I know I did when I woke earlier.

Looking down through blurry eyes, I could tell I was naked and that I seemed to be lying in a mud puddle. Great, not only was I beat to a pulp and left outside somewhere but I'd been the victim of a clothes-jacker.

My name is Cam Derringer. I'm a private investigator working out of my small but cozy office-slash-houseboat in Key West. I was investigating a boat theft ring which has been running a very successful business in the Keys. I guess somewhere along the way I missed something. Not a first.

Don't get me wrong. I'm not without my skills, but I do have my faults. Probably my biggest is my size. I'm six foot four inches tall and weigh two hundred and thirty pounds. Mostly muscle. I work out daily and try to stay in shape. I guess I'm doing okay for fifty-two, but I'm no problem for a couple of twenty-something heroes trying to impress their friends or just prove to themselves how tough they are, although I have taken a few of them down.

But that's not what happened this time. I never saw who hit me. The first blow was to the back of my head, not hard enough to knock me out but plenty hard enough to render me helpless from the barrage of punches and kicks that followed. The last thing I heard was, "Back off or you're a dead man," yelled into my ear.

That was going to be a problem; but right now, I had a bigger one. I'm out in the country somewhere, naked. I painfully turned over and got myself to my hands and knees. My knees hurt from the rocks on the road. I think maybe whoever dropped me off here didn't stop the car first.

I looked around and saw I was lying in the middle of a wet dirt road. Tires had rutted it from past rain and neglected maintenance. Recent rain had filled the ruts with water. Vegetation shouldered both sides of the road and grew close to its edge. It left little room for a vehicle to miss me if one came along. I guess whoever did this thought, what the hell if he gets run over then problem solved. I guess it had rained since I was dropped here because I remember my clothes being wet.

I got to my feet just in time. I could see headlights coming toward me. I took a painful step to the side of the road, and a truck slowed down and stopped beside me.

"Help me please, will you?" I said in a very raspy voice. I think I must have taken a punch to the throat.

The truck was a red and rusty Chevy S10. The wheels were covered with mud which left a perfect arch from the front wheel well up the fender, across the door and then widening to cover the entire side of the bed. The driver flipped on a spotlight and pointed it my way, blinding me. My eyes felt as though someone had thrown acid in them. The guy sat silently for a second before laughing and speeding away. The truck bounced over the rutted road. One tire would find traction and throw a rooster tail of mud before the other took its turn. The truck then fishtailed and threw a blanket of mud at me. I couldn't move quick enough and was hit in the chest with rocks and mud. I could hear him laughing until he rounded the bend in the road and disappeared from view. The truck left a trail of blue smoke that made me even more nauseous than I already was.

"Thank you," I whispered, as loud as I could.

Nice guy; can't even help a man when he's injured.

I started walking in the direction the truck had gone. I figured there had to be something in that direction. I didn't know where I was or even which Key I was on. I could smell myself, and it wasn't pleasant. I had blood dripping from my mouth, leaving a metallic taste. A full moon lit the night, and a slight breeze actually chilled me.

Chapter 2

Another set of headlights came from behind me, a few minutes later. The car slowed and stopped across the road from me. It wasn't muddy like the truck; only the tires and a small amount around the wheel well. I surmised that it hadn't been out in the rainstorm. They must be from around here.

"Help me, please," I whispered.

"Stay where you are," a young female voice said. "Who would you like for me to call?"

Smart girl, I thought, helpful but cautious.

"Call Diane for me," I said, gratefully. I gave her the number and could see her dialing.

I fell back to my knees and held my arm again, knowing I was going to be in serious pain for a long time.

"She's on her way, sir. She's bringing clothes. Can I do anything else?" the girl said, apprehensively.

"No, but thank you very much," I managed through the pain.

"You must have really pissed someone off," she said, now matter-of-factly.

"Yeah, I do that sometimes."

I felt myself getting weak again and fell back down on my side. The young woman got out of her car and came to me.

"Are you sure you don't want me to call an ambulance?"

"No, I'll be fine," I gasped. "Where am I?"

"Cudjoe Key. I'll stay with you until she gets here."

"Thanks."

She knelt down next to me and placed her hand on my arm. Her touch was soft and comforting. It actually relieved some of the pain. She was good.

"Do you know who did this to you?"

"I have no idea."

"Did you know they painted a mustache on you and wrote 'kick me' on your forehead?" she giggled but then said, "Sorry."

"Jeez, how embarrassing. I'm laying here naked with graffiti all over me, in front of a beautiful young lady, and I don't even know your name."

"Jenny," she said, restraining a giggle.

"Nice to meet you, Jenny. I'm Cam," I said through the pain.

"I'll be right back," and she returned to her car.

She came back with a pink sweater and laid it over my mid-section.

"You looked like you might be more comfortable with this," she said.

"Is pink all you have?" I asked, trying to break the tension.

"Sorry, Cam," and she put her hand on my arm again, but then my world went black once more.

Chapter 3

I woke again. The bright lights were blinding so I closed my eyes. I could hear voices. One belonged to Diane but the other I didn't recognize.

"Will he be alright?" Diane said, in a low whisper.

"He'll be sore for a while, but we didn't find any broken bones. There is a small laceration to his right bicep. Looks like someone tried to cut it with a rusty blade of some kind. We cleaned and bandaged it and gave him a tetanus shot. That should hold him for a few days, and then you can change his bandage."

"Okay, if he'll let me. He's kind of hardheaded."

"I can hear you," I said.

"Cam, you're awake," Diane said, surprised.

"Yeah, and it sounds to me like you're worried."

"Not me. I just didn't want to have to spend all day here signing papers," she said, nonchalantly.

"I knew you cared."

"Doctor, is there anything you can give him to put him out again?"

"Mr. Derringer, can you open your eyes?" The doctor asked.

"I can, but the light is too bright, so I think I'll just keep'm closed for a while," I said, trying to sound like W.C. Fields for some stupid reason.

The doctor walked across the room and dimmed the lights.

"Try now if you don't mind."

This time it was bearable but not pleasant. I could see Diane and the doctor looking at me, but there were four of them.

He took a small light and shined it in my eyes. "They look clear enough. I don't see any permanent damage, but his vision will be foggy for a few days. Are you going to be able to stay with him for a while after we release him?" he said, turning to Diane.

"I guess I can check in on him once in a while."

15

"Thanks for your concern, Diane," I said in a weak sarcastic voice. "You have plenty of work to do at the office anyway."

"Okay, since I'll be there anyway, I'll look in on you once in a while."

"Fine," the doctor said and left the room.

I surmised, by the "LKMC" on the Doctor's coat, that I was in the Lower Keys Medical Center.

"How's the young lady who was with me when you arrived?" I asked Diane, still in a whisper.

"She was fine, but you were naked—big shock."

"Oh, you noticed, huh?"

"I said, 'shock'."

"Oh, I thought you said..."

"I know what you thought I said. Anyway, she left as soon as she helped me dress you, and after I'd called an ambulance. And you have been written on."

"Yes, I heard about that."

"Mustache, 'kick me' and a phone number on your, uh, big shock."

"A phone number on me, down there?" and I pointed at my cock.

"Yes, in lipstick."

"You didn't wipe it off, did you? Evidence you know."

"No, we were going to copy it, but we need to wait until the rest of the numbers are showing. You know, when you are feeling better, and stronger."

"Funny. I wonder why she left? She seemed to be sincerely concerned."

"Maybe she got to know you better."

Diane and I talk like this all the time, but we really do care for each other. She is my secretary-slash-accountant-slash-advisor-slash-everything else she thinks I need. She's only thirty-two, but very wise in the ways of the world. She has a Doctorate in Psychiatry and practices it on me constantly. Her father was my partner in a law firm that ran into a bit of trouble. He was killed; I was disbarred. Her mother died in a car crash a year before that.

My wife Malinda and I took Diane in when she was fifteen, and she has been with me ever since.

For the past five years, my wife has been missing. We had a good marriage, but she just disappeared without a trace. I did the usual search for her, and then five times more. If she were out there on her own, I would have found her. I suspect foul play was involved. She was out on her boat when she disappeared. It was found six months later in a boatyard in the Bahamas. That's when I started my investigation on the boat-jackers. I'll never quit searching for her.

Diane's a very beautiful, five foot two inches of dynamite with blonde hair to the center of her back. It keeps me busy just screening the boyfriends. Now she's seen me naked, I will never live this one down.

"Do they call you Derringer because of the small gun?" Diane said.

Here we go.

"Wait until I feel better at least. Don't kick me when I'm down."

"But the sign says, 'Kick me'," she said, holding her fingers up in quotation marks.

I laughed. "Ouch! Don't make me laugh," but then the door opened, and Sheriff Willie Buck walked in.

Chapter 4

Sheriff Buck was a slightly overweight man who had been in Key West for about ten years. He'd helped me in my search for Malinda, but without any luck.

His large frame and rough voice usually forced confessions from criminals without even needing to touch them.

"Well, Derringer, you really pissed someone off this time," he said in his gruff voice. He rested his hand on the nine-millimeter he carried in a western-style holster tied to his leg.

"Hello to you too."

"Did you get the number of the truck?" Buck asked.

"I think it was a tank. Anyway, it hit me from behind. I never saw it."

"Who do you think would want you killed, or maybe warned?"

"Lots of people, unfortunately."

"Cam, you live by the gun, you die by the gun," he said. It was his favorite saying, and I'd heard it on more than one occasion.

"It was probably just someone who needed a nice suit," I joked.

"I can see you're not going to help me find the guys. You need to be more careful. One of these days I'm going to be looking down at you in the morgue."

"I'll let you know if I find out who it was. I'll deliver them to you myself."

Looking at Diane, Buck said, "Try to talk some sense into him. It's for his own good."

"I'll try, but you know how that goes," she said.

"Keep an eye out for my billfold. Driver's license, credit cards and all that," I said.

"See ya' round, Derringer. Call me if you need me," and Buck tipped his hat to Diane as he left.

Diane left the room too. She said she was going to get a drink and would be right back. I took the opportunity to pull the sheets back to see if I really had a phone number on my cock. I did. I couldn't see well enough to read it, and it did look like a few numbers weren't visible. Someone was really funny. They knew I would have to be erect to read the whole thing, but how did they get it written on there in the first place?

I pulled the covers back and looked up. Diane was watching me.

"Can you read it yet?" she said, raising her eyebrows.

"No, but if I could get a little privacy, I might be able to."

"And a magnifying glass."

"No, it's just that my eyes are blurry."

"The first five numbers are 351 66," Diane said.

"How do you know that?"

"I read them."

"Jeez."

"Don't be so modest."

"Wouldn't you be?"

"Yes, but you're a dirty old man."

I spent the night in the hospital.

The next morning, Diane showed up with some clothes for me. She helped me dress and waited with me for the doctor.

He gave me a prescription for Percocet.

A nurse wheeled me to Diane's car, and together they helped me in.

The weather was muggy as usual, but the sun was shining, and it was a beautiful sight. It was nice to be a free man again.

We stopped on the way home at CVS and filled the prescription. I took one immediately.

The houseboat-slash-office was located at the end of a dock that held five other houseboats. Diane opened the gate, which had a chain and lock hanging on the rusted bars. The hinges squeaked when she pushed it open. That was about the amount of our security—a warning squeak. The lock hadn't been used for years. I'm sure it would take a cutting torch to open it now.

"Hey, Cam, what happened to you?" came the voice of Stacy. She and Barbie lived on the first boat. Both were in their mid-thirties. They worked as waitresses at Coyote Ugly, proving the name of the place very misleading.

"Nothing, I just slipped," I said back to her in a whispery voice.

"Let us know if you need anything."

"Thank you, I will."

"You'd like that wouldn't you?" Diane said. "Two gorgeous blonds in bikinis waiting on you."

"Maybe they could read the number."

"I think it was put on there by the girl who helped you. The lipstick matched."

"Really?"

"Yep."

"Interesting. She saw the big gun and wanted me to call her."

We passed the other boats, but no one seemed to be home. They usually weren't. They were owned by snowbirds that came down here to escape the frigid temperatures of home.

I had to step up to get on my boat. Not such an easy task for someone in my condition. Diane had spent the night here and had cleaned the place up. She had the refrigerator stocked with food and beer. There was a bottle of Wild Turkey sitting on the table next to my chair and some beer in the fridge for her.

"I turned your bed down. Would you like for me to help you in?"

"No thanks. I'm going to sit out back, have a drink and ponder the situation for a while."

"I don't think that's a good idea with the Percocet."

I gave her the look.

Diane fixed me a drink, opened a beer and joined me on the fantail-slash-patio.

"Thank you."

"You're welcome," she said.

"I think whoever did this had something to do with the boat-jackings."

"Probably, but there are other people who have a score to settle with you too."

"Yeah, but they said back-off. I'm not pressuring anyone else right now."

"Were you close to something there?"

"I was just getting close. I think it's all drug-related. These guys are hijacking boats and using them to smuggle drugs. After they're delivered, they take the boats somewhere else and sell them on the black market. Then they get new paint and numbers and are sold at seemingly legitimate boat sales."

"Can you prove any of this?" she asked.

"No, not yet. It's just a theory right now."

"And the previous owners, what happens to them?"

"Overboard is my guess."

"You're thinking about Malinda, aren't you?"

"It could have happened to her. I hope not."

Chapter 5

The next morning when I woke, I actually felt a little better. I was still sore but could manage to get up on my own and go to the bathroom. I must have been feeling better because I could read the rest of the phone number. I got a pen from the nightstand and copied it down.

I showered and went through the living area to the kitchen, still naked, to get some breakfast.

"Oh, I see you're feeling better this morning," Diane said.

"Whoops, I didn't know you were here."

"Did you write it down?"

I covered myself the best I could with my hands and backed out of the room. "Yeah, I got it covered."

"Not all of it," she teased.

I dressed and went back in the kitchen where Diane was making breakfast; bacon and eggs, toast and coffee.

"Perfect. Smells delicious," I said.

We ate on the patio and made small talk about the weather.

She asked how I was feeling.

"Better, sore but better."

"Are you going to call the number?"

"Yes, I am. I don't know what it's about, but I need to know. It could have something to do with what happened to me."

"I think it has something to do with what is going to happen to you."

"Either way, I need to know."

I dialed the number. A lady answered on the third ring.

"Hello," she said in a sleepy voice.

"Hello, this is Cam Derringer. Who might I be speaking to?"

"Well, Cam, I guess you're feeling better, or you wouldn't have my number," now in a very sexy voice.

"Is this Jenny?"

"How many girls do you pass out in front of?"

"A few, but you're the only one who has ever left their number on me. How did you manage to do that?"

"I had to stretch things a little. With a little coaxing, it cooperated."

"You're an interesting girl, Jenny."

"If you ever feel like company, call me. I can make you feel better," she said in a sensuous voice.

"And if I call you, what would I use for a last name?"

"You can use Jacobs."

"Will do. Bye for now."

She said, "Goodbye," and hung up.

"You were right. It is something that is going to happen to me," I said.

"Only you could get a date while passed out. You're something else."

"Thank you."

Chapter 6

I went back to my desk, retrieved my notes from the last three years, and returned to the patio.

"I had to have missed something. I was prepared for trouble, but not from behind and not yet. Someone I trusted must have been working with them."

"Maybe they saw you asking too many questions too many times," Diane said.

"Could be."

I called Jack Stiller, my partner, and confidant on this case. He was a top-notch investigator. I got no answer.

"I'll try him again later. Must have had a hard night."

He had been known to stay out a little too late and party with the ladies. Once, when we were working on an infidelity case, he went missing for three days. Turned out he was in Vegas with the woman he was hired to tail. Luckily, her husband never found out. It turned out he was having more affairs than she was, and he was physically abusive to her to boot.

I went over the rest of the papers. Nothing really jumped out at me. If it were the Mexican Cartel, I probably wouldn't be able to do anything anyway, but also, if it were them, they would have killed me, not warned me.

I heard the gate squeak and felt footsteps on the dock. I closed the folder and dropped it into the live well beside my chair. I always protected my paperwork.

"Good morning, Derringer," Sheriff Buck said.

"Good morning, Willie. Like some coffee?"

"Naw, it's official. I need all your notes on the boat-jacking cases. I know you've been working on them, and so does the FBI. They say you're getting in their way and they want you to back off."

"Back off? Was that their exact words?"

"That's what they said. You want to get those notes."

29

"I don't have them. Whoever did this to me ransacked my boat and took them."

"Cam, if you don't give them to me, they'll come and get them. They let me come as a favor," Sheriff Buck said.

"Really, I don't have them."

Willie looked at me for a minute and then at Diane. "You couldn't talk any sense into him I guess."

"He's like a closed door," she said.

"Okay, Cam, I'll tell them you got robbed. You had better hide them before they get here, though. If you decide to come to your senses, give them to me, not the FBI.

"Why would I do that?"

"Because if they get them they'll be gone and we'll never solve the mystery."

"Sure you don't want any coffee?"

"I'm sure. I'm already too jittery. Oh, and by the way, I have something for you."

He pulled my wallet out of his pocket and handed it to me. "One of my men found it along Blimp Road, close to where you were found."

"Thank you," I said and took the wallet.

I looked through it. The money was gone, but the cards were all there.

"Well, that saves me a lot of trouble. Your man didn't steal my money did he?" I asked, grinning.

"No, but you can make a claim. How much did you have?"

"Let's see," I said. "Including the twenty I had hidden behind my license, I would say, twenty-two dollars."

"I'll see you later. Bye, Diane,"

"Goodbye, Willie," Diane said.

"Thanks again," I called after the sheriff as he left.

I took the case notes back out and looked at them again.

"I wonder why they really want me to 'back off'?"

"You're in their way."

"Those are the exact words the thugs who beat me used."

"So you think the FBI had you beaten and warned to back off,"

"Yeah, I kind of think that. If they did, they'd be real sorry. I'll make their lives miserable."

"I don't like the sound of that. You know you can't go up against them."

"Would you mind taking the notes home with you?"

"Why not," she said. "I might as well be on the top ten most wanted with you."

"Thank you. You are a good sport."

31

"Okay, I have some work to do and a few patients to see this afternoon. If you need anything, call me."

"Thanks, Diane, I love you."

"I love you too, Cam," Diane said and kissed me on the cheek.

"Here, don't forget these," and I handed her the notes.

She took them and left.

Chapter 7

I called Jack again; **still no answer.**

I decided to go into town and revisit the scene of the crime, taking my Mercedes SL 350 to Front Street where I parked. I walked the boardwalk to the marina and down to the slip where the boat was docked a few nights ago. The slip was empty. A forty-two foot Sea Ray had been parked there the last time I was here. It matched the description of one reported missing in Marathon Key a few weeks ago. The numbers and the name had been removed. I was sure it would have new ones by now. Last week, while I was looking it over in the dark and jotting down a description, I was whacked from behind and thrashed.

I looked around the docks but didn't see anything or anyone out of the ordinary. The boat already had a search posted for it, so it wasn't going to do me any good going to the police. If it turned up, I would know. I have people.

While I was down here, I decided to go to Sloppy Joe's and have a drink. It wasn't very crowded this time of day, and there were no cruise ships in port.

I took a seat near the open windows so I could watch the street and the people in it walking by.

"Here ya go, Derringer," a young and very charming waitress said as she set down my Wild Turkey.

"Thank you, Tanya. Join me?"

"I'll be right back."

Tanya returned a minute later with her own drink. She had her thick brown hair tied back in a ponytail. Her large breasts were spilling out of her sheer white tank top, and her mini dress left little to the imagination. Still, I imagined.

I had helped Tanya out of a jam two years ago. She sold Marijuana to an undercover agent and was busted. She was looking at five years in prison. I might have lost my law license but not my pull.

Since Tonya was a friend of Malinda's, I pulled a few strings and got her off with community service. As far as I know, she has been on the straight and narrow ever since.

"So, Cam, what happened to you? You look a little weathered," she said, looking at the cuts and bruises on my face.

"I had a run-in with some ghosts. At least, I couldn't see them."

"I think you should go back to practicing law."

"I would if they would let me, but they won't."

"That was a bum rap. You should still be practicing, and Jim Dade should still be alive," she said.

"I agree, especially about Jim."

I had been watching the sidewalk and noticed a girl pass by on a bicycle, looking a lot like Jenny. "JENNY!" I yelled, but she didn't hear.

"You know that one?" Tanya asked.

"Kind of, I think. She helped me out of a jam the other night."

"She's been hanging around here for the last week or so. Been asking a lot of questions about the docks. Says she is going to buy a new boat and wants to make sure it will be safe leaving it here."

"Really, she has money? I wouldn't have thought."

Chapter 8

I left Sloppy Joe's and drove around town a little, looking for Jenny. There was no sign of her, so I decided to return to my boat. Her bicycle was leaning against my gate.

Stacy came out to her sun deck when she heard the gate.

"Hey, Cam," she said. "You've got company. She's hot."

"Thanks for the warning. I'll take it from here."

Stacy was pretty hot herself in that micro bikini.

I stopped at the gangplank and looked around the boat. Jenny was sitting on the patio, sipping on what looked like a Wild Turkey.

"Jenny?"

"Who were you expecting? You saw my bicycle," she said with a crooked little smile.

"How was I to know that was your bicycle?"

"Because you yelled at me when I rode past Sloppy Joe's."

"Oh, so you did hear me."

"I didn't want to disturb you and your girlfriend."

"My *friend*. And she says she knows you."

"I've talked to her a few times."

"What are you doing here?"

"You may come aboard, you know. I came to see how you were. So, how are you?"

"Not bad, considering," I said, wondering how to play this. She had seen me naked, so I didn't have any bargaining chips to play. Everything is out in the open, so to speak.

"How did you know where I lived?" I asked.

I sat down in the chair closest to her and could smell the sweet fragrance of her perfume. Now I had a better look at her, she was quite stunning. She had short black hair and ample breasts, the first two things a man notices. She also had a seductive smile. I guessed she was about five foot six inches tall.

"Did you get the phone number washed off?"

"Yes, I had to scrub it for a while, but it finally came off."

"You want me to reapply it?"

"Maybe another time. I'm not quite strong enough yet."

"Too bad. I was going to write you a note this time."

"Tanya tells me you're in the market for a boat."

"Yes, I am. I've just moved here from Michigan. I had to leave mine there. I can't live without one."

"I'll be glad to introduce you to a friend of mine who owns a boatyard and does yacht sales."

"That would be great. Thank you," she said, smiling.

"Mind if I ask what you do for a living?"

"Nothing anymore. I did run a very successful hedge fund. I got out while the getting was good."

"Smart lady."

My cell phone rang, and I excused myself and stood to answer.

"Hello."

"Mr. Derringer?"

"Yes, this is he."

"My name is Susan Crane. I understand you're a private detective."

"Yes."

"I would like to talk to you about finding my husband."

"Do you live in Key West?"

"Yes, we do."

Although I would like to spend all my time searching for the men who might have taken my wife, I needed an income too. The creditors like it when I pay my bills.

"Give me your address and a time I can come and talk with you," I said, pulling a pen and a scrap of paper from my pocket.

She gave me an address on White Street and asked if I could come around one-thirty.

"I'll see you then," I said, hung up and sat back down.

"Sorry about that. Business."

"Anything important?"

"Just a new client. Needs some legal help."

"So, you're a lawyer."

"Not anymore. Used to be."

"A used-to-be lawyer. What does a used-to-be lawyer do when he's not a lawyer any longer?"

"I'm a private investigator."

"Oh, that explains the shape you were in when I found you. Someone was mad at you. Was it a jealous husband?" she said, raising her eyebrows.

"I don't know, but I doubt it. More likely a nervous boat-jacker."

"Is there a problem with that down here?"

"Not a big one, but enough that you should be careful. You shouldn't go out by yourself too often."

"I guess you'll have to go with me then. I don't know any other big strong men."

"I'll be honored to protect you on occasion."

"Thank you."

"I have a few things to do today, but if you would like to join me for supper tonight, I grill a mean steak," I bragged.

"I'll bring the wine."

"Perfect."

She leaned forward and kissed me softly on the lips. I could feel a stirring down deep inside. We stood, and I walked her to her bicycle.

"You don't have a car?" I asked.

"I have a car. I prefer a bike when I can, though."

"How green of you."

"Whenever I can."

She rode away, and I watched until she was out of sight. Very pretty, but why was she in Cudjoe Key in the middle of the night?

Chapter 9

I ate a sandwich and washed up, changed clothes and drove to White Street. Mrs. Crane's house was on a corner, surrounded by a three-foot high white picket fence. Flowers adorned the sidewalk and the boxes under the windows.

I rang the doorbell. It was answered by a woman in her late sixties with gray hair pulled back too tightly in a bun. She was tall for a woman and still had her schoolgirl figure.

"Mrs. Crane?" I said.

"Mr. Derringer, please come in," she said, stepping aside for me to enter.

"Thank you. Just call me Cam," I said.

The house was bright for a conch style home. Big windows, which I could tell weren't original, let in plenty of sunshine. The furnishings were modern, and it was very stylishly decorated. Large Oriental rugs covered the old wood floors.

"Have a seat," she said, motioning me toward a large wingback chair.

I took a seat, and she offered me some coffee or tea.

"No thank you. I just finished lunch."

"Well, I guess I should just get right to it then. My husband William—we call him Bill—has been missing for three weeks. I went to the Sheriff's office, but they didn't have any luck finding him. I don't think they even tried."

"It's not easy to find someone unless they turn up dead. So it's a good thing they haven't found him."

"Yes, I guess you're right if you look at it that way."

"Where did you last see him?"

"We had breakfast, and he kissed me goodbye and left for work like every other day. That was three weeks ago tomorrow."

"Where does Bill work?"

"He's an independent insurance investigator. He has an office in the Conway building on Outer Flagler Avenue."

43

"Was he working on a case at the time he disappeared?"

"He had several going. He always did. One was a man suing a trucking company for running into the back of him at a stop sign. He said something about a stolen painting from the museum and a stolen boat up in Marathon Key."

That one set off alarm bells in my head. Looking for stolen boats had become very dangerous.

"May I go to his office and have a look around?" I asked.

"Yes you can, but the Sheriff already took a look. He didn't find anything. That was about all he did."

In my opinion, the Sheriff never does more than is necessary.

"May I ask how you came to call me?"

"I remember you from your court days. You were quite the attorney. I saw your name in the phone book and thought, if you were as good at being a detective as you were a lawyer, I would take my chances with you."

"Thank you for that. It's good to receive praise once in a while."

"You should still be a lawyer. That was a bad deal, and I know you did the right thing."

"Yes I did, but not in the eyes of the bar examiners."

She gave me the address of Bill's office and the keys. I left and drove straight to his office. It was a large building with ten suites. Bill's was upstairs on the end.

I inserted the key, but the door was unlocked. Leave it to the sheriff's office to leave the door open. I pushed it open and stood back instinctively but heard nothing from inside. No one shot at me so I assumed it was safe.

Turning on the lights, I had a look around. The office was furnished sparingly but efficiently. There was a large desk in the center toward the back, four padded chairs facing it, the same number of file cabinets on the left and a bookshelf on the right. There was a small refrigerator with a coffee pot on top.

I walked around to the back of the desk and sat down. I found nothing of interest in the drawers; maybe even a little too neat. I lifted the desk mat and peeked under. There was a handwritten note. It said, "Follow the money circle."

I stuck it in my pocket. I needed to think on that for a while.

Opening the file cabinets, I looked through the new case files. Here was the one on the motorist suing the trucking company. I studied it. It seemed the poor guy had a case. I wrote down his name and number to call him later.

The stolen art from the museum had been appraised at twenty-five hundred dollars. I had never heard of Sabena Larue, the artist. The price was probably inflated, but I didn't think that was enough to kill a man over.

That was it. There was no file on a stolen boat in Marathon. Someone had beaten me to it.

I stood in the center of the room, trying to pick up on the vibes, wondering what he'd been feeling the last time he was here. I held my arms out in a Jesus like stance and closed my eyes. I tried to envision the room through my third eye, the way they taught me in yoga class. It didn't work. It never did.

I decided to give Sheriff Buck a visit and so drove to his office.

"Well, Cam, have you come to your senses?" is the way he greeted me as I walked in.

"No, not yet. This is on a different case I have recently acquired. I believe you have been working on it."

He looked at me defensively. "What case is that?"

"Missing person, William Crane."

He flinched. It didn't go unnoticed.

Chapter 10

"Yes, we have a bulletin out all the way to Miami for him. He just disappeared. Why does this interest you?"

"His wife Susan has hired me. I went to his office today. The door was open. Did your men maybe forget to lock it?"

"I doubt it. We don't work like that," he said, puffing his chest out in a self-justifying manner.

"I thought maybe we could team up on this one. She seems like a nice lady. I'd like to get her husband back," I said, thinking I could catch more flies with sugar.

"Yeah, me too, but you know as well as I do it ain't gonna happen."

"Maybe, but I feel like I should try. Do you have anything that might help me?"

"Noda."

"Did you question the museum or the car accident he was working on?"

"Sure did. I don't see any reason either one of them would have to kill him."

"No, me either. What about the boat theft he was working on, up in Marathon?"

"Don't know anything about that other than Susan said there was one. I guess you think it is related to the other case you're working on."

"Don't know; none of it makes sense yet. I'll let you know if I find anything. I hope you'll do the same," I said, knowing we were both being insincere.

"Sure will, Cam, but if I were you, I wouldn't spend too much time on it. When people are missing that long, they usually show up in the morgue."

I left and drove to the store to get a couple of T-bone steaks. I grabbed a few potatoes and some green beans. I thought that would do it with the wine. With wine, everything tastes good.

Once back home, I marinated the steaks in my special sauce, covered them and let them sit.

I fixed a Wild Turkey and got out my notepad. The note from Bill's office fell out with it.

"Follow the money circle."

I laid it aside and jotted down a few thoughts.

Why did Buck flinch; where was the file on the missing boat; why did someone jump me, maybe nothing to do with this case, but really, coincidence? And why was Jenny in Cudjoe Key? Jenny probably had nothing to do with this, but that's the way I think.

The time was getting away from me, so I made a note to call Marathon tomorrow and find out more about the missing boat.

I started my Green Egg grill and took a shower. When I got out, I changed clothes three times before settling on a Rum City Bar T-shirt and cargo shorts. Flip-flops topped off the wardrobe. I was trying to show her how we dressed for supper down here in the Keys. Looking in the mirror at myself, I felt I had done it. My once dark brown hair now had a hint of gray in it. It was a little long, just covering my ears. My mustache had worked its way down into a slight Fu Man Chu. I grabbed my electric trimmer and leveled it out to the corners of my mouth again. I still had a strong jaw from working out and really had no noticeable wrinkles. My nose was okay. It had been broken a few times, but I only had a slight bump on the bridge.

49

I started a slow cook on the green beans, put the potatoes on the grill, and picked up my guitar. This was one thing I always enjoyed. Playing guitar and writing songs. Although I wasn't exactly a good singer, I could play the guitar.

Jenny showed up at seven o'clock wearing a Jimmy Buffett T-shirt and shorts. "I hope I'm not late."

"Not at all," I said. "I've just been enjoying the evening. I'm afraid I started drinking without you, though."

"Not to worry, I brought reinforcements," she said, pulling a bottle of wine from her purse.

I picked it up and read the label, "My compliments to the barkeep."

"I was hoping you liked red."

"Red before bed, white before light."

"I've never heard that one before."

"I know; I just made it up. I've been writing songs tonight and was still in the rhyming mood."

"You'll have to play something for me later," she said, kissing me softly.

"I plan to," I said, returning her kiss.

The potatoes were ready, so I removed them from the grill and opened the vents to increase the temperature to five hundred degrees.

"How do you take your steaks?" I said.

"Medium well please."

"Same here."

I put the steaks on and opened the wine to let it breathe. Two minutes on each side and then I closed the vents to allow the steaks to bake.

I removed them from the grill and placed them on the table. Jenny had the salads ready along with the beans and potatoes.

"Good teamwork," I said.

"I knew we'd be good together," she said with a sly smile.

The meal was delicious, and so was the company.

"You're good at this. I guess you give all the girls this treatment," she said, digging for confirmation that she was special.

"Actually, this is a first for me. Since my wife went missing five years ago, I really haven't dated much. I went out for a few dinners, but nothing came of them. You are the first to visit my humble abode."

"Wow, talk about pressure."

"No need to feel any. I haven't anything to compare you to."

~*~

We had a wonderful evening. We drank our wine while cuddling on the chaise lounge and watching the stars. We talked about everything and nothing.

Around midnight, she said, "I think I should go now."

"You can have your choice. Either you can take the bed, and I'll sleep on the couch, or I can call a taxi. I really don't want you to drive after drinking. It is late," I said firmly.

"Okay, I'll take the bed. But I want you to join me," she said, turning to see the expression on my face.

I was torn. I wanted her, real bad, but I didn't feel right. It was like deciding that Malinda was never going to return. In my heart, I knew she wasn't.

"Can I take a rain check on that one?" I said. "I need to talk to myself first."

"I understand. You sleep on the couch."

"Thank you," I said, and then we kissed.

Lying on the couch that night, I thought about Malinda. I still remembered what she was wearing the first time I saw her—and the last.

We met at a party when I was attending Yale University. She was in town visiting her cousin for the weekend.

I was dancing with another girl, and drinking beer as I did when I made a beautiful move and spilled it right on Malinda's head. She got up from her chair and threw her own beer in my face. We stood there, glaring at each other, both of us dripping beer. Finally, I reached out my hand and said, "Nice to meet you. Do you come here often?" We both started laughing, and the rest was history.

I wonder what she would think about Jenny being here? I'll never know.

Chapter 11

The next morning I felt myself being shaken awake. I slowly opened my eyes and saw it was Diane.

"Why are you sleeping on the couch, Cam?" she said.

I sat up and looked around. Everything had been put away and the bed, which I could see from the couch, was neatly made.

"Couldn't get comfortable so I thought I would camp out," I said, realizing that Jenny was gone.

"I'll fix you some breakfast if you want to shower. You smell like perfume."

I showered, shaved and then returned to the living room where Diane was setting omelets and bacon on the table.

54

"Coffee or juice?" she asked.

"Both."

"So, who was the lucky girl?" she said, smiling at me.

"What makes you think there was a girl?"

"This note that says, "Thanks for the wonderful night. See you soon.""

"Oh, that girl. It was Jenny. I made supper for her to thank her for helping me."

"Good for you. It's about time."

"Nothing happened."

"Still, a step in the right direction."

I ate my breakfast and drank my juice before speaking again.

"I miss Malinda," I said softly.

"So do I, but it's been five years, Cam. It's time to start a new life. You deserve it. You did all you could."

"Yeah, I know you're right, but it still hurts."

She reached out, took my hand and just held it. We didn't speak for a long while.

"So, what's new?" she asked, breaking the silence.

"I got a new case."

I told her about Mrs. Crane and the sheriff's blundering investigation.

"That doesn't sound like the sheriff's office. They always seemed to do a halfway decent job," Diane said.

"Yeah, halfway decent. It's like they don't really care if this one is solved."

"What's the next move?"

"I'm going to Marathon today to talk to the local police. I want to find out all I can about any recently stolen boats. I'd like to talk to the owner of the one Bill was investigating. There are no records here, only his wife saying he was on the case. Maybe someone there filed an insurance claim."

"Maybe I should go with you?" Diane offered.

"No, I can handle it. I'm feeling pretty good now. I'm just a little sore."

"Let me change your bandage before you go."

She did, and I was grateful. The last thing I needed was an infection. The wound was healing nicely. She placed the new bandage on and kissed it. I thanked her and told her it felt better already.

"You can have the day off if you like," I told her.

"Not really. I have some scheduled appointments today. You know a girl has to work at a job that pays too. I can't donate all my time."

"Oh, I see. Now you're going to start asking for pay."

"No, of course not. I figure you paying for my education was enough."

"That was money your dad had put away for you," I said guardedly. I wasn't sure how much she knew. I thought she might just be guessing.

"Cam, I know we're just kidding, but I know my dad lost all his money in the ploy that got him killed. I know you and Malinda are the ones who paid for my education. I found out two years ago. I love you for doing that, and making me think it was my dad."

"I didn't know you knew. Your dad did have your college money put aside. He had to use it but thought it would be returned in a few days. Then he was killed, and the money was gone. It was the least I could do. I owed him that much."

"You were a good friend to him and like a father to me," she said putting her hand on my arm.

I hugged her. "You've been a good daughter to me."

We stood there for a minute just looking at each other.

"Well, I guess I better get going. I'll be back tonight," I finally said.

"Be careful. This sounds like maybe there is some foul play going on.

Chapter 12

I left the boat and headed to my car.

"Hot chick last night," Barbie said as I passed their boat.

"And this morning," Stacy said.

"Thank you for noticing," I said and kept walking.

I was thinking about Jenny as I sat in the northbound traffic jam, so I gave her a call.

"Cam, do you miss me already?" she said.

"Actually, I do."

"What are you doing today?"

"I'm leaving for Marathon. I'll be back tonight."

"Business?"

"Yes," then I paused for a minute. "Would you like to go along?"

"I thought you'd never ask," she said excitedly.

~*~

She gave me her address. I told her I would be there in ten minutes.

I pulled up to a neat little house she was renting on South Street. She was standing on the front porch waiting for me. Today she was dressed in a very sexy blue flowered dress and white sandals.

"You look lovely," I said as she got in the car.

"Thank you. You dress up very well yourself."

We headed north on the Overseas Highway. It was a magnificent day for a drive. Of course, having a stunning girl in the seat next to you didn't hurt anything either.

"I need to stop in at the police department for a few minutes. I'll be glad to drop you somewhere if you'd like, and pick you up later," I said.

"I wouldn't mind going with you if it's okay."

"No problem. Just thought it might not be your cup of tea."

~*~

A young man in uniform greeted us at the front desk. He didn't look old enough to be a policeman.

He did a double take on Jenny and smiled. Maybe it was a good idea to bring her with me.

"May I help you?" he said, looking directly at her.

She looked at me, deferring the answer.

"Maybe," I said. "My name is Cam Derringer. I'm a private investigator from Key West."

His eyebrows rose.

"I was hired by a Mrs. Crane to find her missing husband. He is an insurance investigator and is working on a case here, involving a stolen boat. I was wondering if you might have reports of any lately."

He opened a book that was lying on the desk next to him and paged through it.

"Looks like four in the last couple of months," he said, closing the book.

"I wonder if I might be privy to the names of the owners and any other information you might have on these cases."

"No," he said dismissively.

"Captain?" Jenny said in a soft southern voice I'd never heard before and offering a sensuous smile, "I know it isn't customary for the police department to share information with just anyone who walks in here, but this is a life and death situation. Without your help, we'll never be able to find this poor man. His wife is worried sick."

"It's Sergeant, ma'am," the officer said, smiling and puffing up a little. "I guess it wouldn't hurt to let you see the reports."

"Thank you very much. That would be a great help," Jenny said and smiled at me.

He handed me the book, never taking his eyes off Jenny.

Two of the reports filed were on twelve-foot johnboats. One was on a pontoon. The last was the one I was looking for. It was a forty-two foot, Sea Ray. Just like the boat I was looking at when I got clobbered.

Its owner, Gary Bartley, reported the boat stolen six weeks ago. It was fully insured, and a claim had been filed with Florida Key's Mutual two weeks ago. I wrote down Bartley's address and phone number.

When I looked up, I saw Jenny standing close to the desk. The sergeant had moved around it and taken a seat on the edge. He was so occupied, I could have taken the whole book to his printer and copied it. Jenny saw I was finished and moved a step away from him and broke the spell.

"Thank you again, sir, for your help," I said, laying the book back down on the desk. "I'll let you know if I find out anything."

Jenny handed him her card and said, "Would you mind calling me personally if you discover anything new on this case." She let her hand linger in his as she released the card.

"Yes, ma'am, I will. You can count on it."

"Thank you. It was a pleasure meeting you."

Chapter 13

We walked back to the car, and I opened the door for her. "That was a marvelous piece of flirting you did in there," I said.

"It looked like you needed the help. I don't think he liked private detectives."

"They never do."

"Where are we going now?" she asked.

"We're going to the Florida Keys Mutual Insurance Company in Islamorada. I want to find out more about a claim on a stolen cruiser. It sounds like the one I was looking at when I was attacked."

"Whose boat was it?"

"You ask as many questions as I do."

"Well, if I'm going to be your partner, I need to know what's going on."

"My partner?"

"Yeah, how much do you pay?"

"Pay? I don't pay my partners. They usually work pro-bono, just for the pleasure of being with me."

"Well, I do like being with you. Okay, I'll work for free," she said, using her southern accent again.

She extended her hand to me. I took it, and we shook.

We drove north toward Islamorada. On the way, I called my real partner, Jack Stiller. Still no answer. I must have had a frown on my face.

"What's wrong?"

"My partner, Jack. I haven't been able to get in touch with him ever since I got out of the hospital."

"Is that unusual?"

"Yes. He calls me every day to check-in."

"Where was he the last time you talked to him?"

"He was going to the marina to talk to the security guard."

"Why don't you call them and see if he showed up there?"

"I think I'll pay them a visit in person. I like to see their faces when I ask questions. You can tell a lot from a man's face."

We found the insurance building and pulled into the lot. It was a three-story, white stucco structure.

"Would you like to wait here or come with?"

"I'd like to come with. I am a partner now. But I need to make a phone call first."

"You go right ahead. I'll be inside," I said, getting out of the car. I couldn't help but wonder who she was calling. She was a mysterious woman.

I entered the building into a small vestibule that housed a gray-haired woman behind a large desk that almost took up the whole room.

"May I help you?" she asked.

"I hope so," I said with my most charming smile. "My name is Cam Derringer. I'm a private investigator. I've been hired to find a missing person. I think you might know of him. He has done work for this office in the past."

"A missing person? Who is it?" she said with an astonished look on her face. Most people who don't deal with this type of thing fall into a type of bafflement and even mild shock. It's best to strike before they come around.

"William Crane, a private insurance investigator," I said.

"Oh no, not Bill," she said in disbelief. "He was such a nice man."

She used the past tense. She already had him dead.

"When was the last time you saw him?" I asked.

"Well, I think about three weeks ago. He had an appointment with John Trapper. That's who he always dealt with here."

"Is Mister Trapper in?" I asked, still smiling at her.

"Yes, just a minute and I'll page him."

She did so and told him he had a visitor in the lobby.

"I'm sure he heard the page. He'll be down in a minute. I hope nothing bad has happened to Bill," she said, now coming a little more to her senses.

"Me too. How well do you know him?"

"Only what I know from our short talks here while he waits for John to come down."

I knew I wasn't going to get anything else out of her now.

Jenny came in a minute later, picked up a magazine and thumbed through it while we waited for John to appear. I was afraid I had made a mistake asking her along on a business trip. I knew she had no interest in watching me ask questions. I would have to do something nice for her when we left here.

Mister Trapper came down the stairs and stepped into the lobby. He was a tall and very heavy man. Not a muscular heavy, but a fast-food heavy man. He shook my hand with a weak, feminine grip.

"Mister Trapper, my name is Cam Derringer. And this is my associate, Jenny Jacobs. I represent Mrs. Crane, Bill's wife. Do you have a minute to talk?"

"Sure, right this way," he said.

He led us into a small office off the vestibule and closed the door behind us.

He offered us a seat and asked if we would like something to drink.

"Not for me, thank you. How about you, Jenny?" I said.

"No thanks, I'm fine," she said.

"What is this about?" he asked.

"Mister Crane has been missing for three weeks. His wife says he was working on a case that involved a stolen boat. The records at the local Police station show that someone from this office was handling a claim on it."

"We handle a lot of claims in this office. I don't recollect any particular claim involving a stolen boat."

"The man's name is Gary Bartley. He filed the claim five weeks ago on a forty-two foot Sea Ray. The name was 'COUNT ME INN.' I believe William Crane was investigating that claim. Your receptionist says you always worked with Bill. Is that right?" I asked, pointedly.

"Mister Derringer," he said, accusingly, "are you insinuating that I might have had something to do with Bill's disappearance?"

"Not at all, I'm just trying to follow his footsteps the last day anyone saw him."

He looked at me and then at Jenny, then back at me. "I don't think this is anything we should be discussing. How do I know you're not after Bill. I don't know that he is missing."

"You may call his wife if you wish. She'll be glad to tell you," I said, pushing his buttons a little harder.

"Look, Mister Derringer, I know all about you. How you and your partner tried to set up those drug dealers, so you could have them captured by the police. Something you shouldn't have done since you were defending them. Your partner ended up dead, and you disbarred. While I think it's a good thing the serial killer-slash-drug dealers ended up dead also, I don't believe you are a man I want to be involved with. Ethics and all, you know," he said sarcastically.

"Mister Trapper, as of now you are involved with me," I said, trying to intimidate him.

It worked a little but not the way I had hoped. He got to his feet. "We are finished here. If you need anything else, please inform our legal department."

"You sound like a man who has something to hide. I'll be in touch with you," I said and got to my feet, took Jenny's elbow and steered her toward the door.

"Mister Derringer," Trapper said, "I hope you find Bill. He's a good man."

"I will," I said, and we left.

Chapter 14

Once outside, Jenny said, "Well, that went well."

"Better than you might think," I said. "He knows something. He might not know where Bill is, but he knows who does."

We got in the car, and I put the top down. "It's a beautiful day. Why don't we enjoy it?"

"I already am," she replied and kissed me.

A red Mustang was sitting at the end of the parking lot. The driver started his engine and followed Cam. He stayed a safe distance behind so as not to be spotted. He picked up his cellphone and made a call.

"Mister Derringer just left John's office," he said to the man on the other end.

"Follow him. Is Jenny with him?"

"Yes, she is. They seem very cozy together."

~*~

"Well, where are you going to take me now?" Jenny asked.

"I thought we would go to Marathon and talk with Mr. Bartley. Let's see if he really wants to get his boat back."

"Oh, Cam, you know all the fancy places to take a girl," she said, again in that southern drawl.

"Don't fret; I'm going to treat you to a wonderful lunch first."

"Good, I'm getting hungry."

We drove to Marathon, and I turned into Key Colony and drove to the Key Colony Inn.

"Here we are, the best lunch in town. You may have anything you wish from the lunch specials."

"Why thank you, sir."

We went in and were seated by the window. The place was very tastefully done and the menu opulent.

We ordered, and each chose a glass of wine.

"So, Jenny, if I'm not being too nosey, may I ask where you are from and why you chose Key West to settle in?"

"Not at all. I'm originally from Fort Collins, Colorado. I stayed there until after I graduated from college and then took a job in St. Joseph, Michigan. Eventually, I took charge of a Hedge Fund. I felt it had run its course, so I resigned, with benefits. I finally got tired of the cold winters and decided to go as far south as I could. Now I live three blocks from the southernmost point."

"Are you planning to remain retired or are you going to start another hedge fund?" I pried.

"Well, now that I work for you, I don't have time for a Hedge Fund."

"What am I going to do with you?" I said, shaking my head.

"I can make some suggestions if you can't think of anything," she said with a sly smile.

Our food came just in time. We busied ourselves with small talk as we ate.

"May I ask where you are from and why you chose Key West?" she asked.

"Touché," I said. "I am from Key West. I went to college at Yale, came back here and wouldn't live anywhere else."

"Was your wife from Key West also?"

I felt a familiar pang, as I always do when someone speaks of Malinda in the past tense.

"No," I said. "I met her while in school. We married when I graduated, and she moved here with me."

I guess she saw the pain on my face. "I'm sorry, Cam, I didn't mean to pry."

"That's okay. No harm in asking questions. After all, if you're going to be a private eye then you have to ask questions."

We were quiet for a few minutes, and I looked out the window again. The red Mustang was still there. I had spotted it first when we entered the insurance building in Islamorada.

"You don't have a boyfriend around here do you?" I asked.

"No, I don't. Why?"

"That Mustang has been following us all day. Someone is nervous."

Jenny looked out the window at it. She leaned back a little and slid slightly away from the window as if to hide.

"Do you know the car?"

"No, I've never seen it before."

"I'll get behind it when we leave and run the plates."

We finished our second glass of wine and left. Once in the car, I swung wide around the lot and got the plate number.

I called Sheriff Buck and asked if he would run it for me.

"What are you up to, Cam?" he said.

"Just curious as to who has been following me all day."

"I'll get back to you," he said.

I drove slowly out of Key Colony. It was the wise thing to do after two glasses of wine. They don't take to speeders in this town.

I turned left onto Highway One and drove toward Sombrero Beach Road.

The Mustang which was following me out of Key Colony turned right.

"Well, I guess he got tired of us," I said.

"We are kind of boring," Jenny joked.

My cell phone rang.

"Hello," I answered.

"Cam, are you sure you got the plate right? This number doesn't register," Sheriff Buck said.

"I think so. He stopped following us just now. If he comes back, I'll check it again."

Chapter 15

"Okay, let me know," he said and hung up.

I turned left again on Sombrero Beach Road, drove to the first right and turned into a golf community. Bartley's house was halfway around the street and on the water.

I asked Jenny to stay in the car this time. "I'll be right back. You never know how you'll be greeted without an appointment. I don't want anyone punching you in that pretty little nose," I told her.

"I'll be waiting for you," she said.

I walked to the massive front door and rang the bell. A minute later, a man in painters' coveralls answered the door.

"Can I help you?" he said, sounding annoyed.

"Yes, I would like to speak to Gary Bartley please."

"Mister Bartley doesn't live here anymore," he said in an impatient tone.

He opened the door wider and said, "Look at this place. He destroyed it before he left."

I looked inside. He was right. Some walls had "Kiss my ass bank" spray-painted on them, and others had holes kicked in them. Lights and appliances were gone.

"Did he leave anything behind? Personal stuff?" I asked.

"Nope, not a damn thing."

I thanked him for his time and went back to the car.

"It looks like Bartley lost his home to the bank. What do you want to bet he was losing his boat too when it turned up missing?"

"What are we going to do now?"

"I guess we'll go home and regroup."

We went back to my boat. We thought sitting on the patio and having a Wild Turkey might help us think.

When I opened the gate, it squeaked. Stacy came out and called to me.

"Cam, you had visitors while you were out. Two big guys in suits," she said.

"Thanks, Stacy," I said and drew my gun.

"Jenny, will you wait here for a minute? I need to check this out."

"Sure, no problem," she said.

"Jenny, come on up on my boat and wait. They're gone, but it will be safer anyway," Stacy said.

Jenny did.

"Thanks, Stacy," I said.

I walked cautiously to my boat. The dock squeaked and bounced as I walked. I willed it to be still, but it didn't cooperate. Many times I welcomed the warning it cast off, but not now. When I was where I could see on board, I could tell the boat had been searched.

Whoever it was didn't bother to put anything back. Chairs were overturned, and books were off the shelves. The bed was stripped and the mattress on the floor.

I didn't know what they were looking for, but I bet they didn't find it, then remembered the files Sheriff Buck had come after. He'd said the FBI would come for them.

I stepped into the cabin with my gun at arm's length. I felt something beneath my foot, stepped back and looked down. It was a glass unicorn. I had given it to Malinda one year for her birthday. We had spotted it in New York in a display window at

Saks Fifth Avenue. She had a fit over it, so I went back later that day and bought it for her.

Now it was broken. I'll get whoever did this, I promised myself.

I picked it up and tried to piece the parts back together. It looked like they would fit. I placed it on a shelf for safe-keeping until I could get some super glue to repair it.

The bedroom looked like a bomb had gone off. My good bedside lamp was broken and lying on the floor. There was no need for that. Whoever did this was trying to send me a message.

The worst part, though, was all the holes in my walls. Someone had taken a hammer to them all. Assholes.

I went back outside and called to Jenny. She came to the boat and looked in from the dock.

"We need to call the sheriff," she said.

"Yeah, I guess we do. There's a lot of damage in here. I'm going to have to turn it in to insurance."

"Who do you think did this?"

"Maybe the FBI. Sheriff Buck said they would come for my files on these boat jacking cases."

"Why would they want your files? Is there something in them that would interest them?"

"I guess they think so," I said, looking around again at all the destruction.

I called the sheriff while Jenny walked through the disaster area.

"He's on his way. He doesn't sound too happy with me, though. He said 'I told you so'."

"He told you the FBI would do this?"

"Well, not exactly this, but he did say they would come for the files. He came to get them from me, but I told him I didn't have them."

"Where are they?"

"My friend has them. Diane, you met her."

"Yes, I hope she's not in danger."

"Good thought, I better call her."

I called Diane and told her about the boat. "I think you better return those files to me tomorrow. I don't want them coming to you for them."

"Okay, Cam, but I'm going to copy them first and put the copy in my safe deposit box."

"Good idea," I said.

"I'll be there in about an hour. I want to see the boat."

"Okay, but it's not pretty."

"It never was," she joked.

Chapter 16

Sheriff Buck arrived about twenty minutes later.
It was starting to get dark, and I saw his flashlight
coming down the dock. Barbie heard the gate
squeak and came out on her deck.

"Hiya, Sheriff," she said.

"Hello, Barbie," he said, tipping his hat.

"I'll get the lights for you."

She walked to the gate and flipped a switch on
the post. A string of party lights came on and lit the
dock.

"Thanks," the sheriff yelled back at her.

He came to the boat and looked around. "I don't
think the FBI did this. When I told them you didn't

have the files they said they would get a warrant and force you to hand them over."

"Maybe this is the way they force people," I said.

"Who else would want those files?" he asked.

"I guess the guilty party."

"And who is that?"

"I don't know, but someone is nervous. They beat the shit out of me and have now ransacked my boat. Someone thinks I'm close to something."

"And you're not?"

"Maybe; I don't know."

He filed a report and took some pictures. Before he left, he asked me one more time for the files.

"I swear I don't have them."

"But you do know where they are, don't you?"

"I could probably find them if I wanted to."

"Find them before you get killed."

"I will."

"Were there any witnesses?"

"Stacy saw two big guys in suits."

"I'll talk to her on the way out."

He left, and I started picking things up and trying to put my life back together.

Diane arrived a few minutes later. She and Jenny pitched in, and we had the place looking livable again in a few hours.

"Thanks, ladies," I said. "Now I would like to take you two to supper."

"It's pretty late, but I could eat something, and maybe a drink," Diane said.

"I don't have any other plans. Why not," Jenny said.

We all squeezed into my Mercedes and went to old town.

Duvall Street was packed. It usually was at night. We walked down to the Hogs Breath Saloon. It appeared there was standing room only, but I know people. We were seated in just five minutes. It was a miracle.

We ordered drinks and appetizers. The entertainment was top-notch, as usual.

"So, what do the two of you think? Would the FBI do something like this?" I asked them.

Diane said, "From what I've seen on television shows they would. But then, that's TV."

"No way. They know they would be exposed and open for a lawsuit. I think it's either a robbery or whoever has something to hide," Jenny said.

"Either way, I'm going to find them," I said firmly.

Our appetizers came, and we busied ourselves devouring them.

"I was hungrier than I thought," I said, sticking a chicken wing in my mouth.

"Yeah, me too," Jenny said.

Diane didn't say anything. She just looked at us with a potato wedge sticking out of her mouth. We all laughed.

Two men entered the bar and stood at the end. They looked out of place. They weren't drinking or even smiling. They looked around the room and finally settled their eye's on our table. I returned the stare. They broke off first, acting as though they weren't interested in us, but I knew they were.

I started to rise, but Jenny took my arm and pulled me back down.

"I saw them too," she said. "Let it go for now. This isn't the time or place to accuse anyone. Not in a bar. A bar fight can turn ugly."

I looked at the wall behind them and saw that the web camera was on. It ran most of the time. They were right in front of it.

"I'll leave them alone, but excuse me for a moment," I said and stood.

I went to the manager who was a friend of mine. "Jerry, how you doing?" I said, smiling.

"Fine, how about you? Wait, that was a stupid question, seeing the girls at your table."

"Life is good," I said. "I wonder if you would do me a favor."

"Sure, which one do you want me to take? Diane, I hope," he said, grinning.

"You just keep your hands off of Diane."

"Whatever."

"I would like a copy of the last ten minutes of the webcam. Can you do that for me?"

"For you, sure," he said.

"Thanks, I owe you one."

"Which one?"

I just shook my head and walked back to the table. I could feel their eyes on me. I stopped and looked back, directly at them. They looked away uncomfortably. *Idiots.*

Chapter 17

We finished our drinks and rose to leave. I turned and mock-saluted the two men at the end of the bar. This time they didn't look away. I could see the steam coming off them. I might have pissed them off.

We returned to the boat and Diane kissed me on the cheek and left.

"Would you like a nightcap?" I asked Jenny.

"How about a rain check? I have a few things I need to do, and it's getting late," she said, apologetically.

"Not a problem," I assured her. "I'll take you home."

When we arrived, I walked her to her door and kissed her goodnight. I felt like a high school boy again. Once she was safely inside, I walked back to my car.

A red Mustang was parked down the street. I could see the two men inside watching me and was sure it was the same car from earlier, and the same two men from the bar. This time I was prepared. I drew the gun from my waistband and aimed it at them. The car roared to life, they slammed it in reverse and burnt the tires trying to get away. I wanted to shoot at them, but they hadn't done anything wrong.

I went back to Jenny's house and knocked on the door. I could hear her on the phone.

". . . and two goons watching us from the bar. What the hell was that . . . I have to go. Someone's at the door."

When she opened the door, I acted as though I hadn't heard the conversation.

"Jenny, the two men from the bar just made an attempt to attack me. Luckily, I was ready this time. I thought I had better see if you wanted me to stay with you for a while or if you wanted to come with me. I don't know if they'll return."

She looked out the door, up and down the street. "Are they gone? Are you okay?"

"Yes on both counts. But I'm worried about you."

"I doubt if they'll be back. You probably scared them, and they know we'll be looking for them. I'll be okay."

"Okay, but call me if you hear anything. I'm only moments away."

She kissed me again and said, "Be careful. We don't even know what these guys want."

I drove back home the long way, zigzagging around town to see if I was being followed. The conversation I'd overheard kept going through my mind. Who had she been talking to? Whoever it was, they were privy to our situation. Was it the same person she had called from Islamorada?

Back at the boat, I poured another Wild Turkey and sat outside with the lights off for a while. I tried Jack on the phone again. Still no answer. Now I was really worried. So far Jack, Bill Crane and maybe Gary Bartley were missing. What, if anything, does Jenny have to do with all this?

~*~

"The boss wants to talk to you," Ronnie Pierce told Billie Daryl and handed him the phone.

"Yes, Juba," Billie said into the phone.

"Did you get him?" a rough voice said.

"Not yet. I sent two good men, but he had a gun."

"And they didn't?"

"Didn't think they needed one. He surprised us."

"God Damn it, Billie. Am I going to have to do it myself? He's getting too nosy. Do you want to go to the gas chamber? You should have taken care of him when you dumped him in Cudjoe."

"Don't worry. We have it under control," Billie said, defensively.

"It doesn't sound like you do. You better take care of this soon, or I'll be looking for some new partners. Live ones," the boss said and slammed down the receiver.

"Damn, Ronnie, I think Juba might be a little pissed," Billie said, laughing.

"Yeah, maybe we should kill him too. He can join the party at the bottom of the sea."

They both laughed.

Chapter 18

My phone rang early the next morning. I couldn't decipher the noise at first. I sat up, put my feet on the floor and looked around. My head hurt a little, and I remembered having too many drinks the night before. I picked up the phone.

"Hello," I said, trying to sound as if I'd been up for hours and just finished my workout.

"Mr. Derringer?"

"Yes, Mrs. Crane. How are you this morning?" I said, recognizing her voice.

"I'm okay, but I'm still worried. I think you should come by again today. I have something I want to give you," she said, almost in a whisper.

"I can be there in about an hour."

"That will be fine. I'll see you then," she said and hung up.

I sat on the side of the bed for a moment and made a promise to God that I would never drink again; at least not that much.

I stood and walked to the shower. The water ran cold for about thirty seconds before it started to heat up. I took a little of the cold before enjoying the heat. I let the water run down the back of my neck, and I lightly massaged my aching muscles. I showered until the water started to get cold again. I felt much better already. Maybe I'd been a little hasty with my prayer.

I thought oatmeal and orange juice sounded like a good way to start the day. I put a couple of slices of bread in the toaster and pushed down the lever.

My automatic timer on the coffee pot hadn't come on yet, so I flipped the switch on and walked out to the patio, to check out the new day.

An empty Wild Turkey bottle sat on the table. Under it was a piece of paper. I lifted the bottle and picked it up. Written in what looked like a child's printing was a note.

"Back off or join Jack!"

Join Jack. What the hell happened to Jack. I tried his number again. This time the phone was answered. "Let it go, Cam" was all that was said, and then the line went dead. It wasn't Jack's voice.

~*~

I ate a couple of bites of breakfast and called Jenny to see if she was okay.

"I'm fine, Cam. I told you they wouldn't be back," she said.

"Just checking. See you tonight?"

"I guess so. What are you doing today?"

I didn't want to tell her about the note or about Mrs. Crane calling. I needed to figure out if she had any connection to all of this first. I hoped not.

"Oh, just some errands. A few loose ends on another case," I said. "Then I need to go workout."

"Good, I want you to keep that body looking good for me."

"That's the plan."

"Why don't you come over here for supper tonight? I'll show off my cooking this time."

"Alright. I'll bring the wine this time."

"See you around six," she said, and we said goodbye.

~*~

I pulled up in front of Susan Crane's house. The front door was open. I drew my gun and walked slowly to the porch. Standing beside the door, I took a quick peek inside. I could see Susan lying on the floor. I stepped inside and surveyed the room with my gun. No one was here, and the house was quiet.

I went to Susan and felt for a pulse. She was alive and starting to stir.

"Mrs. Crane, are you okay? Can you hear me?" I said, placing my hand on her cheek.

She looked at me. It took a minute for her to focus.

"Mr. Derringer. Did they take the folder?" she said.

I looked around the room and saw no folder.

"Where was it?" I asked.

"On the coffee table," she said weakly.

"I'm afraid they did. Lay still, I'm going to call an ambulance."

When the medics put her in the ambulance, they said she was still conscious and talking. They didn't think she appeared to have any major injuries, but they needed to check her over at the hospital.

I searched the house for the folder after they'd left. I found none. I wondered what was in it that was so important that someone would do this for it. In the master closet, I found some very expensive clothes; five pairs of women's Manolo Blahnik shoes.

I picked up a pair of men shoes, to read the label. Louis Vuitton; Christ, these things sold for around ten thousand. How in the hell could they afford this?

Silk suits hung next to fashion designer dresses.

I needed to see their financial records.

I leafed through the desk in his home office and found what I was looking for, an American Express Centurion Card. I used to own one. Now I couldn't even pay the annual fee.

I copied down the numbers and the code on the back, wiped it off and returned it to the drawer. These people had some serious money. Either they'd won the lottery, or they did something besides investigating insurance claims.

Whatever they did, they'd have to keep a low profile, but he must have gotten in over his head on something because now no one knew where he was.

I found another drawer in which there was a file. It contained a list of stolen boats. I looked through to see if anything rang a bell. The list went way back.

The column on the left had the registration numbers next to which came the size and make, then the name, with a dollar figure down the right.

"FL 4098 LP – 24FT. – OFFSHORE – LADY A – $25,000".

The list went on like that. I scanned the names.

I came to the one I was looking for.

"FL 6253 LP – 34FT. – MERIDIAN SEDAN – MY MALINDA --- $175,000".

My heart sank just reading that name on someone else's files, and that boat was worth at least $250,000 five years ago. I ran the list through the printer on the table and returned it to its hiding place.

I was about to leave when I heard the front door open. I could hear two men talking. They were coming toward the office.

I hid in the closet and waited, expecting to be caught. They turned on the light and went straight to the desk.

"I'll get the files and check the safe for the key to the box," one man said.

"Okay, but make it quick. We don't want anyone to find us here," the other man said.

"Someone's been here," the first one said. "My files are gone."

Son of a bitch. It was William Crane. He wasn't missing, he was hiding.

"Gone. How can that be?" the other said.

"You need to find Susan and ask her what happened to my files," Bill said.

"But she'll know I've been here if I do that."

"Tell her you need them for a case you're working,"

"Okay, I'll try. Get the key from the safe for the money and let's go."

I recognized the other voice now. It was John Trapper, the insurance man from Islamorada.

I chanced a peek through the slats in the door. I could see Bill as he went across the room and moved a bookshelf. Behind it was a safe. He opened it and removed a small box containing a key. Probably a safety deposit box, I thought.

He closed the safe and returned to his desk where he pulled the file of the boat listings I had copied.

"At least we have these," he said.

They left.

Clearly, they didn't know Susan was in the hospital, so they didn't have anything to do with that.

Now, this was a whole new case. I wasn't looking for a missing person any longer. Now I was looking for a man on the run.

As soon as I heard the front door close, I ran to the window to see the car. It was a white Cadillac SUV. I didn't have a good view of the plates, but I reasoned it was probably John's.

I left Mrs. Crane a note on the table, asking her to call me. I didn't really know what else to do. I decided I would check with the hospital later that afternoon.

Chapter 19

Jack Stiller sat in a hard wooden chair in the bedroom of Juba's house. His hands were tied behind his back, and he had a gag in his mouth. His eye was swollen and his nose broken from the continuous beating he had been taking.

He wasn't usually this easy to take advantage of. His six foot six frame and gym induced muscles made it difficult for someone just to grab him and tie him up, but this time he'd been suckered in by a beautiful face and a hot body.

He was thinking back to the days before he became an investigator. Selling boats hadn't been such a bad way to make a living. He'd been home every night by six o'clock; free to go to bars and

97

enjoy life, but now he didn't think he would ever be free again. He had seen too much.

He heard the door open and cringed at the sound. This wasn't going to be good. It never was.

"Well, Jack, I'm tired of trying to beat the answers out of you, so I give up," the boss said.

"My friend here is going to take you for a boat ride. If you decide to tell us where the pictures are before he gets to his favorite spot, we'll let you go, but we can't let you go with those pictures. I don't want to do this, Jack, but I will. So please tell us."

He pulled the gag from Jack's mouth. "Well?"

Jack looked at him and smiled. "If I die, the pictures go to the police."

"No, they don't. You didn't have time for that." The boss paused for a moment. "Ronnie, take him out to the special place you took Gary Bartley and drop him off if he doesn't talk. Make it tonight, and take the girl with you. I want her to do it. Use her boat."

"Yes, sir, my pleasure."

The cell phone rang, and the man they called Juba looked at the caller ID.

"Excuse me," he said to Ronnie.

He turned and left the office. He didn't want Ronnie to know too much.

"Yeah," he answered.

"It's John," the caller said. "I was with Bill all day. I don't think he knows any more than what was in his files."

"We have that file, John. Does Bill have any idea where the boat records are?"

"Yeah, they were in his desk. He said there was no copy. How did you get the file?"

"Mrs. Crane was attacked in her house today. Somehow the files ended up on my desk if you know what I mean. She's at the hospital. Go visit her."

"Okay, but what about Bill?"

"Where is he?"

"He's at the Peterson's vacation home. He has a key for it while they're gone."

"Let him be until we're sure there aren't any surprises then we'll decide what to do with him. We really need him for the insurance deals."

"Yes, sir," John said.

The boss hung up and called for Ronnie. "Try to get this son of a bitch to talk before you kill him. We need to at least get one of those files or the pictures. Shit, everything is going wrong all at once."

Chapter 20

I went home to eat lunch. My small breakfast was wearing off fast. After rifling through the fridge, I decided on a big, fat all-beef hot dog. It wasn't bad, but it did make me crave a steak.

I stopped by the hospital to check on Susan after that. The nurse at the desk told me she'd been treated and released about an hour before. I asked her if anyone had picked her up. She checked her board and said a Mr. Trapper did. I thanked her and left.

How did Trapper know where to find her so quickly? Things were really getting complicated. Every time I thought I had something figured out, something else changed.

Now I was more worried about Jack than I was about Bill Crane. If he didn't want to be found, why should I waste my time looking for him?

I went to the marina, the last place I knew Jack had been before he disappeared. He'd said he'd wanted to talk to security there.

I entered the security station and was greeted by Dan Haden, an old friend. We went to high-school together.

"Well, Cam, I haven't seen you around for a while. Where ya been? You missed poker last week," Dan said, sticking his hand out to shake mine. "That piss-head Roy took everyone's money again. I lost eight dollars myself."

Dan was referring to a monthly poker game we'd been conducting since high school. Five of us showed up regularly, and three to four others appeared when they could. We all started school together and have remained friends since.

"Well, last week I was in the hospital, mending, and I've been pretty busy since."

"What happened to you?"

"I was snooping around your docks, looking for a stolen boat, and someone took offense to that. They beat me and left me naked in Cudjoe Key."

Dan laughed. "Sorry, I know that's not funny, but it is kind of."

101

"Yeah, they were real comedians. They wrote "Kick me" on my forehead before they left."

He laughed again. "Sorry, but shit, Cam, how do you get into these situations all the time?"

"Don't ask me. Trouble seems to find me everywhere I go."

"Well, what are you here for now. Just a visit or are you trying to find out who wrote on you," Dan said and couldn't resist another laugh.

"I'll save the best part of that story for the card game. If I told you all of it, you'd be useless to me now."

"Can't wait," he said.

"I'm looking for Jack. I haven't seen him since I got out of the hospital. Last we talked, he was coming down here to talk to you. Did he ever show up? It would have been four days ago."

"Yeah, he was here. He was asking me about that forty-two foot Sea Ray docked in B18. Said he thought it was stolen."

"What did you tell him?"

"I told him the guy pulled it in and asked me to watch it for him for a couple of days. Gave me five hundred dollars and I never saw him again."

"What did Jack do then?"

"He said he was going to go over to the Schooner bar and wait for someone to show up. He had his camera with him and was going to get some pictures of the guy."

"Did the guy show up?"

"Not while I was here, but the next morning, the boat was gone and so was Jack. I figured he got what he wanted and went home."

"That was the same boat I was looking at when I got clobbered."

"So, you think it was stolen?"

"Yeah, I think it was stolen, or maybe repossessed and fake stolen from Marathon. It belonged to a Gary Bartley. He lost his house to the bank, and he has disappeared too."

"Man, a lot is going on with that boat," Dan said, thoughtfully.

"Yep, but right now I just want to find Jack. Let me know if you hear anything."

"I will. Good luck."

I left the dock house and went over to the Schooner. Dave Richards was bartending and not overly busy at the time.

"Hey, Dave, how's it hanging?" I said, regressing every time I spoke with him.

He was a good ole' boy from Indiana. He'd moved here when he was eighteen and had now lived here for forty years, contributing to the Key West residents' reputation for being quirky.

"To the left," he replied, sticking his hand out for me to shake. Just as I went for it, he pulled it back. "Whoa, man, you're losing your speed there, brother," he slanged with a big smile. "Sorry," he said and stuck his hand out once more.

I reached for it again, but he pulled it away at the last moment. "Man, you're slow," he said.

"Enough, dude. I need some info from you," I said in a voice I hadn't heard since the last time I'd had a few beers with Dave.

"Whasup?"

"Was Jack in here about four days ago, watching the docks?"

"Yeah, he was. Takin' pictures with that big-ass camera he's always braggin' about."

"Was he okay when he left?"

"Better than okay I'd say. A beautiful young lady came to his table and sat down. They had a few drinks and left together. Out there," he said, pointing to the docks, "She had a big-ass boat. They got on it and left."

"Were they alone?"

"Think so. She went to the restroom once, and Jack came to the bar and gave me a chip from his camera, to keep for him. Said he'd get it later."

"Do you still have it?"

"Yep."

Chapter 21

Ronnie called Jenny. "Hey sweetheart, I've got a job for you to do tonight. Juba wants you and me to take a little boat ride."

"Does it have to be tonight?" Jenny said, thinking about her date with Cam.

"Yep. We're using your boat," Ronnie said with finality.

"When and where?"

"Be at Juba's dock at ten."

"I'll be there."

Thank god he said we were using my boat, Jenny thought. I was wondering how I was going to get around to that.

~*~

I slid the chip into my computer and hit the keys. The pictures came up. The first was the boat sitting at the dock. The next showed a man stepping onto it. Its angle wasn't right to be able to tell who he was. The next one did show the man's face. It was Ronnie Pierce. He was a dock worker who'd been around for as long as I can remember. The next picture was of another man standing at the boat, talking to Ronnie. I had never seen him before, but he was definitely Middle-Eastern. Iraqi was my guess. Then there were three more pictures of him walking back toward Jack's location. In the last of the three, the man was looking right at Jack as he snapped the shutter. I enlarged that one and printed it off. The next few pictures he took didn't make any sense to me. I studied them for a while. They were just views of the docks, full of tourists, but then I saw something in one of them that sent a chill down my spine. It was Jenny in the crowd, walking toward him and smiling. I printed that picture too and put them both in my folder. I would return to Schooners when I had time and show Dave the pictures. I hoped Jenny wasn't the girl Jack left with.

~*~

John Tripper took Susan Crane home. He explained that he needed Bill's files for a case they'd been working on together when Bill disappeared.

"I'm sorry, I don't have those files any longer. Whoever attacked me took them," she said.

She didn't trust John any further than she could throw him. She had told Bill not to get tangled up with him in the first place.

They had a very good business going on their own. They would find clients who were losing their boats or cars to the bank and, for half the insurance money, make sure the vehicles were never seen again. It was a win-win for both parties. They would then also collect from the buyers. They had made a small fortune before Bill got hooked up with John.

Now there were more people involved, the big boss, whom she never did like, and a few Middle-Eastern guys, and if I'm not mistaken, people are getting killed, she thought.

There are more clients nowadays, just as John promised, but only half the money.

"Aren't there any copies?" John asked.

"No, unfortunately, there aren't. Bill wanted to be able to destroy them quickly," Susan lied. She had copied all of Bills files without him knowing.

She loved Bill and knew he loved her too, but a woman needs insurance.

"Okay, Susan, if you hear anything at all, call me. I'm very worried about Bill. He's a good man. I hope they find him soon."

"Thank you, John," Susan said as she rose to walk him to the door.

He stopped there and turned to her. "I guess I don't have to tell you not to talk to anyone about our, uh, arrangement."

"Don't worry about me. I was here long before you came along, and I'll be here long after you're gone," she said angrily, looking him in the eye.

He leaned back from her a little, like maybe he was a bit scared of her. It didn't go unnoticed.

"And don't think I don't know where the money is going," she said.

She had read the files before they were stolen. Things had taken a turn for the worst. She would never have agreed to let them in the business if she would have known.

"Like I said, some things are better left unsaid," he leveled at her in a threatening voice then left, leaving the door open.

She slammed it shut.

Chapter 22

I got ready for my date with Jenny. Again, I pondered on what to wear. This time I chose khaki slacks and a long-sleeved white shirt. I stopped at the wine store and chose a Louis Roederer Cristal Brut 2005 Vintage. It set me back two hundred dollars. Expensive for my taste nowadays, but not at one time. It used to be one of my favorite vineyards.

I pulled up in front of Jenny's house and shut off the engine. I could see her in the kitchen, stirring something on the stove. Watching her doing such a

109

domestic act, I wondered how she could possibly be connected to any of this. Maybe she wasn't.

She turned, looked out the window and saw me. She smiled and waved.

I waved back and opened the car door as if I had just arrived. She met me at the door. We hugged, and I kissed her, taking in the fragrance of her perfume.

She was wearing a very short white dress. Her tanned legs were quite shapely. The only other thing she had on, as far as I could tell, was a very expensive looking pair of diamond earrings. She was heart-stopping.

"Are you okay, Cam?"

"Oh, yeah. Sorry for staring, but you look absolutely exquisite."

"Why, thank you. You look quite fetching yourself," she said, again in her southern drawl.

The house smelled magnificent. The aroma of Italian sauces mixed with her perfume perked my taste buds to the utmost. It made me hungry for dinner, and for her.

"I brought reinforcements this time," I said, presenting the bottle of wine.

"The opener is in the dining room. I have some stirring to do," she said, pointing to the table.

A white tablecloth adorned it, beautiful crystal wine glasses and alabaster plates with gold trim set intimately at one end.

"You have a beautiful house," I said. When I'd walked her to the door the last time, I had only been able to see into the living room.

"Thank you. I haven't had much time to decorate the way I would like to, but it will do for now."

I poured the wine and took the two glasses into the kitchen. I handed her one, we clinked them and took a sip.

"Wow, this is marvelous," she said.

"It used to be my favorite," I said, a little sadly.

"Thank you for sharing it with me then," she said, clinking her glass to mine.

"It wouldn't be the same, drinking it alone."

We kissed softly and then stared into each other's eyes. She finally broke away, back to her stove and her stirring. "You're going to make me burn this," she said. "Go have a seat; it will be ready in a flash."

It was. I poured more wine while she sat the dishes on the table.

"It smells fantastic."

"Thank you. It's an old family recipe," she said.

We ate and made small talk. It was delicious. She then asked me if I had heard from Jack yet.

111

"No, I haven't. I'm quite worried about him. It's not like him to be gone this long."

"I'm sure he will turn up. From what you've told me, he might just be with a girlfriend, holed up somewhere," she said, placing her hand on my arm.

"I hope so," and wondered if she knew more than she was letting on.

We finished our wine, and she said, "I hope you don't think I'm being rude, but I have an early day tomorrow. I'm going to Miami to look at a boat. It sounds promising."

"Great. What kind of boat is it?" I asked.

"Fifty foot Sea Ray,"

"Sweet."

"Yeah, I hope,"

I helped her move the dishes to the kitchen, and she walked me to the door. I was a little disappointed to leave so early. I had finally realized it was time to resume my life. I had hoped that maybe tonight would have a different ending.

"Good luck with the boat," I said. "Call me when you get back."

"I will. And don't worry about Jack. He'll be okay."

I left, wondering how she knew Jack would be "Okay."

Chapter 23

At ten o'clock, Jenny pulled her forty-foot Baha into the dock at the boss's house. Ronnie was waiting for her.

"Right on time, sweetheart," he said.

"Let's get this over with."

Jenny stayed with the boat while Ronnie went inside the house. He returned with Jack, who was blindfolded, gagged and with his hands bound behind him.

"Help me get him into the boat," he said to Jenny.

She grabbed Jack by the arm and pulled while Ronnie pushed. Jack wasn't going to go easily.

Once on the boat, Ronnie hit him on the head hard enough to knock him out. Jack slumped to the floor.

"Take it easy, Ronnie. You don't want to kill him before we can find out where those pictures are."

"Let's go," Ronnie said, roughly.

Jenny eased the boat out of the canal and into the bay. Once clear of the no-wake area, she opened the boat up.

It was another star-filled night. There was a full moon that allowed them to see the deck of the boat without any lights. Jack was starting to move.

Ronnie was busy tying a concrete block to one of his ankles.

"There ya go, buddy. That should hold you down."

He removed the blindfold from Jack's face. Jack looked down and saw the block. He kicked at it, trying to remove it, panic on his face.

"It ain't going nowhere," Ronnie said, "not unless you start talking. If you do, I'll take it off and let you go."

Jack tried to talk, but the gag made it impossible. Ronnie pulled it out of his mouth.

"What?" Ronnie said.

"Screw you," Jack said and spat in his face.

Ronnie backhanded him, knocking him back down. Jack looked at him and laughed.

"You're all over those pictures. You're going to fry," Jack said, a new flow of blood running from the corner of his mouth.

"Just let him be, Ronnie. We'll be there soon," Jenny said.

Jack turned and looked at her as if he'd just realized there was another person on the boat.

"You," he said. "Why are you doing this?"

"It's what I do," she said. "Things will go a lot smoother if you tell us where the pictures are."

"No way, bitch. You're in them too. Maybe they'll give you two a cell together."

Jenny slowed the boat. "We're here," she said.

"Well, Jack, your ride is over. I'll have to cancel your ticket now," Ronnie said and laughed.

"Help me with him," he said to Jenny.

"No. I'm not going to do this part. It's all you."

Jenny busied herself flipping switches and scanning the ocean for any visitors.

"What's all the noise?" Ronnie said, hearing a hum.

"Pumping the bilges," Jenny replied. "We don't want to sink out here."

Ronnie pulled Jack to the side of the boat. He threw the block over first. It banged the side of the boat.

"Hey, easy on the boat!" Jenny yelled.

"If you would help me instead of acting busy, it wouldn't have happened."

Jack was trying to fight Ronnie, but the ropes held his hands tight behind him.

"Any last words?" Ronnie said.

Jack looked at Jenny. "Please don't do this."

"Take a big breath and hold it as long as you can. This will be over with soon," Jenny said.

With that, Ronnie lifted Jack and dropped him over the side. They heard the splash.

"So long, buddy," Ronnie said.

He turned back to Jenny. "That was fun, wasn't it? Now, why don't we have a little fun ourselves?"

He moved toward her. Jenny pulled a gun and pointed it at him.

"I don't think so, Ronnie."

"Oh, you wouldn't shoot me. I just want to have some fun," he said and moved toward her again.

Chapter 24

Jenny pulled the Baha up to the dock for the second time that night.

She shut it off and tied it to the dock, dreading the conversation that was to come.

The lights were on in the house, so she walked to the back door and knocked. A noise behind her startled her. She turned to see the boss standing there.

"Where's Ronnie?" he said.

She jumped. He was holding a gun. At least it wasn't pointed at her.

"You have anything to drink?" Jenny said.

They went inside. Jenny was uneasy and needed that drink.

The boss went to the bar and poured them both a scotch.

"I don't think I'm going to like what you have to say," he said.

"No, probably not."

He just stared at her, waiting for her to speak.

"After we dropped Jack over the side, Ronnie thought we should have a celebration. I didn't agree with him. One thing led to another, and I shot him in the head and threw him over the side with Jack. I didn't have any choice. I'm sorry," she said, solemnly, bowing her head slightly.

"Did you tie a block to his ankle?" he asked.

"Yes."

Juba just stared at her for a moment. He then started laughing.

"I never did like that son of a bitch. I could just imagine him doing what you said. I bet he was surprised when you pulled that trigger."

Jenny was relieved. She had dreaded telling him.

"He was. And so was I."

"Well, I'm sure he had it coming. I'm sorry I put you in that situation."

"Thank you. I was afraid you would be mad."

"No, not really," he said and fixed them both another drink.

"I think you are going to prove to be a real asset. You are now officially taking Ronnie's place."

"Thanks again," Jenny said with relief in her voice. This might be the break she was looking for.

Chapter 25

My cell phone rang early the next morning. Picking it up, I read the caller ID and smiled. It had been too long.

"Chad, to what do I owe this pleasant surprise?"

"Hey, Cam, how the hell have you been?"

Chadwick Kendall had been my college roommate and fraternity brother. I hadn't talked to him for about a year now.

"I've been doing great," I lied. "Are you still practicing in New York?"

"As a matter of fact I am, but I left Canner and James and opened my own law firm."

"Great, congratulations," I said, feeling like a bit of a failure but still happy for Chad.

"Are you sitting down? I have some great news," Chad said, excitement in his voice.

"You mean it gets better?"

"Sure does."

"Okay, shoot," I said, sitting down.

"Well, I need an associate to work for me, someone I can trust and count on. I thought it over and decided you were the only man for the job."

I went silent. I had lost my license to practice law. I know I told Chad about it when it happened.

"Before you get tongue-tied, I have even better news. I made a deal with the board committee, who needed a favor. If you come and work for me for one year and prove yourself to be, uh, let's say reformed, you will be reinstated and get your license back."

I couldn't be sure I heard that right. I can get my license back? No way.

"Cam, are you there?"

"Yeah, I'm here. Are you serious?"

"Sure am. What do you say? I have a great office for you, and I'm sure you'll be a partner in a couple of years."

"Wow," is all I could say.

"Yes, wow is right. It's a second chance. Not everyone gets one of those."

"That's quite an opportunity you're proposing. Are you sure they will give me my license back?"

"Yep, we have a deal. If they back out they will be the big losers."

"When do you want me to come and meet with you?" I asked, my head spinning a bit.

"I'll consider this our meeting. All you have to do is say yes."

I thought it over for a minute. "I'll have to get back to you tomorrow. That's a big move for me. I would have to leave Key West and live in New York. They are the complete opposite of each other."

"Yes, they are. New York, of course, being the more exciting of the two."

"Maybe, maybe not. It's been pretty exciting around here lately," I said, thinking of all that's happened in the last few weeks.

"Well, think it over and call me tomorrow. I hope you decide to take me up on it. It will be good being together again. And don't forget, you'll get your license back to boot."

"Alright, thanks, Chad. I'll call you tomorrow."

Chad hung up the phone and turned to the two FBI agents standing in his office.

"Is that what you wanted?" he asked them.

Chapter 26

I watched Diane walking toward me, her flip-flops beating a steady rhythm on the wooden dock which vibrated slightly at her steps. She looked magnificent in her shorts and t-shirt. She reminded me of Malinda in her younger days. Always so vibrant and full of life. How could I ever leave Diane? She was just like the daughter I never had.

"Hey, Cam," Diane said. "Why the serious look?"

I guess I was staring at her.

"Just thinking," I said.

"Oh, trying something new, huh?"

123

"Funny," I said. "You bring me breakfast?"

"Of course; it's Sunday isn't it?" and she held up the sack she was carrying and shook it.

For years, we'd never missed a Sunday breakfast together. It was a time for us to talk seriously and ponder on the week we'd had. Sometimes we actually came up with solutions to our problems.

"I'll get the milk," I said.

I went to the galley and got a carton from the refrigerator and two glasses from the cabinet. When I returned to the patio, Diane had the plates I had set out earlier, filled with two huge chocolate cinnamon honeybuns.

"Um, Um," I said. "I think those are bigger than last week's."

"Barry said he held them back for me," Diane said and giggled. "I believe he's going to ask me out when he gets the courage."

"Well, if you turn him down, go easy on him. I wouldn't want to lose this benefit."

We each took a minute to tear off a bite of the rolls and stuff them in our mouths. We smiled at each other and then sipped our milk.

"My favorite meal," Diane said.

"I'd do it every day, but then it wouldn't be special."

"So, what big dilemma do you want to challenge today?" she asked me.

I didn't want to tell her about my offer, but I'd vowed never to hold anything back from her. She did the same, and our relationship has been unyielding because of it.

"Let's eat first," I mumbled through a chocolate-filled mouth.

It was another beautiful morning. We both sat and looked out at the Gulf while we ate.

"You know," I said, "there is nothing to look at out there, but you can't help but stare. What is it with a large body of water that makes you look?"

"It's the nothingness. It frees your mind's eye to see what you want to see without everything else getting in the way."

"Well, aren't you deep this morning," I mused.

She laughed and then turned and stared again.

"But you know, I think you're right," I said.

We finished our rolls in silence, neither one of us taking our eyes off the water.

Diane presently got up and took the plates and glasses to the kitchen and then returned and sat down. She placed her chin on her folded hands, elbows on the table, and stared into my eyes.

"What's on your mind?" she asked.

"Really," I said. "You can tell?"

"I always know."

125

"Okay, here goes."

I told her about my conversation with Chad.

"Cam, that's great. You can practice again," she said, excitedly.

"Maybe, but is that really a big deal. I'm happy here, and I have everything I need. New York would be a rat race."

"You know how much you loved being a lawyer. You couldn't wait to get up in the morning and start the day."

"Yeah, but this is pretty good too."

"Are you just worried about leaving me? Because if you are, I can come and visit you once in a while, and you can come here too. I even have some free time coming up. I'll help you get settled in," Diane said, trying to coax Cam into taking the job.

I stared at her for a moment. "You just want to get rid of me."

"Really, you can tell," and she laughed.

"Okay, I'll think it over. I can probably return in a couple of years and pick up here where I left off."

"It's just that I feel like I'm getting close on the boat theft ring. I feel like I'm giving up on Malinda."

"You can't feel that way, Cam. You've done more than most people would have in a lifetime. I'll keep up with the local happenings and keep you informed."

"We'll see."

Chapter 27

After Diane had left, I did some soul searching. I'd tried hard to find the reason for Malinda's disappearance. I guessed I'd been overly obsessed with it. Realistically, if I hadn't found anything in five years, the chances that I would find something the next day, or the day after, were pretty slim.

I'd give it today and call Chad tomorrow with my answer.

My phone rang. I looked at the ID and answered.

"Jenny, I was just thinking about you," I lied. "How did it go with the new boat?"

"It's a beauty. A lot of money, but well worth it. My agent is negotiating with them. We'll know something in a few days."

"Great, good luck with it."

"Thanks. So, I think I owe you an evening," she said.

"That would be nice, but don't think you have to."

"My pleasure."

"Okay, I'll pick you up at seven."

"Dress casual. We won't be going out."

"Good."

"Bye."

"Bye."

I hung up and thought about Jenny. Did I really want to leave her? Maybe I had better find out more about her first.

I drove back down to old town and had to park in a pay lot. Some days it would have been better just to use my bicycle. That was what most of the locals did.

I walked to Schooners to talk to Dave. I thought I would show him the picture of Jenny and see if she was the girl Jack left with.

Sammy was behind the bar today. He was another interesting character.

Sammy had a long, white and slightly yellow beard. His head was as bald as a billiard ball. He wore a patch over his right eye, but one time I could have sworn it was over his left, and he had a peg leg.

He had a parrot on his left shoulder, tethered with a piece of twine. The parrot's name was Pirate. He also had a patch over his eye. One night he got excited and broke loose from Sammy and flew right into a ladies head, falling into her pitcher of Margaritas.

It was obvious he couldn't see where he was going. Sammy pulled him out of the pitcher and gave him mouth to mouth, right there on the table.

The bird's good eye had seemed to wander a little ever since.

"Hey, Sammy, Pirate. How you guys doing?"

"Fine," Sammy said.

"Awwk, fine" Pirate said in his shrill imitating voice.

It was like talking to Charlie McCarthy.

"Is Dave around?" I asked.

"No, we haven't heard from him for a couple of days."

"Is that unusual?"

"Nah, sometimes he gets a little too high and takes his skiff out and fishes for a few days. He always comes back sooner or later."

"Awwk, sooner or later," Pirate said.

I showed Sammy the picture of Jenny. "Have you seen this girl around here?"

Sammy leaned in for a closer look then pulled his patch up and stared with both eyes.

"No, but if I do, would you like for me to take her home for safekeeping?" he said and laughed.

Pirate laughed too.

"No, that's okay. Will you tell Dave to call me at this number when he gets back?" I said as I pulled my card out of my wallet.

"Okee-dokee," Sammy said.

Pirate imitated again.

I walked back out on the docks and took another look for the forty-two foot Sea Ray. It wasn't there. There was a beautiful forty-foot Baha in the slip the Sea Ray had occupied earlier. It was a transient slip, so that could be anyone's boat. I made a note of the numbers anyway.

There wasn't much more I could do. Just hang around and wait. It made me think that New York might not be that bad of an idea after all.

Chapter 28

I decided, instead of just wasting the day, I would go by Susan Crane's house and see if anything new could be learned.

Her windows were open, and the curtains were softly fluttering in the cooling breeze that had picked up during the day. It looked as though we might get a little rain and possibly a cool-down.

I would have thought, after being attacked in her house, she would have it locked down like Fort Knox unless she knew her attackers.

I knocked on her door. No answer. I knocked again. No answer.

I went to the window on the front porch, stuck my head in and called her name.

"Susan? Mrs. Crane?"

Still no answer.

I looked in again; no sign of foul play. I'd half expected to see her lying on the floor.

I removed a business card from my wallet, held it to the frame of the front door, and eased the door closed on it. She would have to see it when she returned and would know I'd stopped by.

What now? I walked to my car and stood there.

New York? Yeah, maybe.

I returned to my boat, showered, fixed a Wild Turkey and sat on the patio, staring out at the water again.

I'm wasting my life. I wanted to call Chad and tell him I was coming but I had already told myself I needed until tomorrow to decide. "Use a little discipline," I told myself.

I arrived at Jenny's house at seven on the dot. Her windows were also open. The evening had cooled down nicely, and the humidity was low.

Jenny answered the door in a short one-piece dress with a big blue paisley print on it.

"You look very stunning tonight, in a hippy kind of way," I said, smiling at her.

133

"And you also, in an island kind of way."

I had on wrinkled cargo shorts, a tie-die t-shirt, and flip-flops.

"You said casual."

"Yes, I did. Get in here," she said, took my hand and pulled me through the door.

She closed it behind me and pushed me back against it as she pressed her body to mine and kissed me hard on the mouth.

Our breathing got heavier, and we started pulling at each other's clothes. She raised her arms, and I pulled her dress off over her head. I was pleased and excited to see she wore nothing under it.

I kicked off my flip-flops, and she tugged at my shorts until they were gone, then tossed them across the room somewhere. My shirt was pulled off over my head and likewise thrown, this time out the window.

We both turned and looked at it, lying out there on the porch.

We then looked at each other and started laughing uncontrollably, falling to our knees, holding our stomachs. We ended up lying together with our arms around each other. Once we felt our bodies together, we quit laughing and went back into a frenzy of passion.

An hour later, we were sitting on the floor, sipping on wine and munching on bread and cheese.

"Wow, that was fun," I said. "It's been a while."

"Well, you didn't forget anything," Jenny said. "You're a wild man."

"At least I didn't throw your clothes out the window," I said and started laughing again.

We laughed on and off every few minutes whenever we thought about it.

Still naked, we leaned against the wall and cuddled while we drank our wine.

"I hate to bring this up now, but I wanted to talk to you about something tonight," I said.

"You're breaking up with me."

"No, not that."

"You want to move in with me."

"No."

"Okay, I give up."

I told her about the call I'd got from Chad.

She sat quietly for a moment until saying, "You'd be a fool not to take him up on it."

"Yeah, that's what I thought until a few minutes ago."

"Don't let that change your mind. It was fun, but we're talking about your life here. Who knows how long I'll be around, and I love New York. I'll go there once in a while and throw your clothes out the window."

We laughed again, then moved the party to the bedroom for a repeat performance.

Later at her front door, we kissed goodnight.

"I'll think on it tonight and in the morning," I said.

"My opinion would be, go for it," she said. "It's the chance of a lifetime."

I kissed her again and stepped onto the porch, where I picked up my shirt and pulled it on. We laughed again.

It was eleven-thirty when I returned home. The gate squeaked as I opened it. Stacy appeared.

"Home awful late, Cam. Big night?" she said, teasingly.

"Yeah, pretty big."

"Got time for a drink?"

"Why not," and I stepped onto her boat.

"Have a seat," she said, "I'll be right back."

She popped a beer and mixed a Wild Turkey for me. She sat them down on the table, pulled her chair closer to mine and sat down with me.

"So, tell me about your big night," she said.

So I did. I told her about Chad, and I told her about Jenny.

"Wow, that was a big night."

"Yeah, I just hope I don't have regrets about either decision."

"Regrets? You were laid and reinstated. What's to regret?"

"Your right, Stacy. What the hell. I'm going for it."

I leaned over and kissed her. "I'm going to miss you, though."

"Are you going to sell your boat?" she asked.

"No, I don't think so."

"Then we'll see each other again."

"Yes, we will," I said.

I finished my drink and kissed Stacy again. "Thanks for being a friend," I told her.

"Thank you. I always felt safe with you here."

I walked down to my boat. I was too fired up to sleep, so I made another drink and sat on the patio.

I raised my glass to the ocean and said, "To moving on. Right or wrong, I have to do something."

I then raised it again. "To you, Malinda. I will never stop searching. I love you."

Chapter 29

Special agent, Manny Sanchez of the FBI, got a phone call from the Miami DEA unit's Chief Investigator, Roger Powell.

"I've got something here that might interest you," Powell said.

"Give it to me."

"What do I get?"

"Depends on what you've got."

"News on the boat ring, but I want what you've got on the Bartley case."

"Okay," Sanchez said.

"We busted a drug mule last night," Powell told him. "Found him floating around in a twelve-foot johnboat. He had fifty pounds of coke with him. He wants to make a deal. Said he saw a man tied to a concrete block and tossed over the side of a boat. He has the name of the boat."

"What was the name?"

"COUNT ME INN."

"Well then, I guess you know what happened to Bartley," Sanchez said. "That was his boat."

"Yeah, I guess so. Any leads on that case?"

"Only the one you just gave me."

~*~

Sanchez called his field agent in Key West and relayed the message.

"Just as you said," Sanchez said.

"You want me to bring him in," the agent said.

"No, not yet. There are bigger fish to fry."

"I'm working on it."

"Watch your back."

Chapter 30

The next morning, I called New York.

"Chad, its Cam. The offer still on the table?"

"Yeah, but are you sure?" Chad asked.

"I'll come for a week and try it on. If it doesn't fit, no harm no foul."

"Sounds good."

"I'll see you Monday then," and I hung up.

I called Diane and told her first. She sounded excited for me. I then called Jenny.

"I decided to give it a try," I told her.

"That's great, Cam. Just think of the possibilities."

"I have. I think it's time to move on."

"See ya tonight?"

"Sure."

~*~

Jenny got a call from the boss. "I need you to do something for me."

"Okay, what do you need?"

"There's a boat I want you to meet at the marina tonight. I have a package for you to deliver to them. Come over here about four o'clock and pick it up. Meet them at five. They'll be in slip twenty-six, next to your boat."

"I can do that. I'll see you then."

~*~

I spent the day going through my wardrobe. I used to dress quite fine, but now it looked as though everything I owned was wrinkled and worn. I still had a couple of very nice suits and wondered what the style was in New York now. No matter how nice they were, they wouldn't look good if they were out of style.

I flipped on the TV and surfed through the channels until I found a world news station.

I looked at the anchors and at the men's styles when they panned to the stories on the street.

I didn't really see much difference in the suits they had on compared to mine. I guess I could wait until I got there. I would buy a few new ties, but my suits would do for a couple of days.

I called Diane and asked her to meet me at Schooners for a drink around four-thirty. I wanted to see if Dave was back to work yet.

At four, I left home and rode my bicycle to the docks. I was able to lock it to the fence behind the bar and enter through the back. I got a table that offered a good view so we could enjoy the entertainment. The sign said that Daddy Grey was playing here today.

Sammy and Pirate were at the bar again. I didn't see Dave anywhere.

Sammy saw me sitting at the table and came over.

"Hey, Cam,"

"Hey, Sammy, Hey, Pirate."

"Awwk, hey."

Sammy said, "I haven't seen Dave around yet. Seems like we would have heard from him by now."

"Yeah, seems that way," I said. "Well, let me know."

"I will."

I ordered a Pina Colada. They had the best in the world.

Diane showed up a few minutes later in shorts and t-shirt. She turned a few of the men's heads at the bar.

"Oooh, that looks good," she said.

I raised my hand and got the attention of the waitress. I pointed at my drink and held up two fingers.

"You look lovely, as usual," I said.

"I like the way you are complimenting me now that you're going to leave me," she said.

"Just say the word and I won't."

"No way; you're not going to use me to bail out of this. You're going."

"I told Chad I would give it a try. If it doesn't feel right, I'll be back before my fridge can defrost."

"Give it time. It's worth it," Diane said, patting my hand.

Our drinks arrived, and we each took a big sip then both grabbed our heads.

"Brain freeze," I said.

"Me too."

After about a minute, we were able to talk again.

"God, that hurts," she said.

"Yeah, try holding it in your mouth for a few seconds first before swallowing it. That will warm it up a little."

We both took another sip, holding it this time before swallowing.

"Better," she said.

We drank slowly and chatted and talked about the people we saw. It was always fun to try figure out what people did for a living.

"I think that guy is with the FBI," Diane said.

"Yeah, wearing a suit. Dead giveaway."

"There's a ballerina," I said, looking toward a tall, slim lady.

"Could be."

I then saw Jenny walk by with a large satchel.

Chapter 31

"There's Jenny," I said to Diane.

"What's she doing here?"

"I don't know. She's been looking at boats but she didn't say anything about looking at one today."

"You wanna yell at her?"

"No, I don't think so. Let's see what she's doing first."

"You're going to spy on her, eh?"

"Yeah, but not for the reason you think. She was in a picture Jack took the last time he was down here."

"You think she might have something to do with all of this?"

"Don't know. Hope not."

We watched Jenny turn and walk out on one of the docks. She went to the forty-foot Baha that occupied the slip I was mugged at and stepped onto the boat.

"Is that her boat?" Diane asked.

"I don't know. She hasn't mentioned having one."

As we watched, Jenny came out of its cabin, walked to the next boat and stepped onto it. A Middle-Eastern man greeted her, and they disappeared into the cabin on that boat.

"I think that man was also in one of the pictures Jack took," I said.

Another man was waiting inside. He was Middle-Eastern also. He was dressed in black slacks, a white shirt, and a Rolex. Very expensive looking clothes. He reeked of money.

"So, you are the new courier I was told about," he said in an Iraqi accent.

"Yes, my name is Jenny Jacobs," she said and stuck her hand out.

He took it in both his and held it there, staring into her eyes.

"I am Amar Mustafa," he said, shaking her hand and then releasing it.

"Asalamu Alaikum ya, Amar," Jenny said.

"Wa alaikum assalaam ya, Jenny," Amar returned.

"Do you have my package?" he said to her.

She reached into her satchel.

A second man reached inside his coat, pulled a revolver and pointed it at Jenny.

"Slowly," he said.

She carefully pulled out the package and held it out for Amar to take.

"Very good," he said, taking it and setting it on the table.

He pulled a knife from its holder on the counter and cut the tape holding the package's wrapper.

He opened the wrapper and exposed a large stack of hundred dollar bills.

Jenny caught her breath. Amar looked up at her.

"Yes, it does take your breath, doesn't it?" he said and turned back to the money to count it.

When he'd finished, he smiled. "Very good. Four-hundred-fifty thousand. It is all here. Would you care for a drink?" he asked Jenny.

"Yeah, I think I could use one," she said.

He opened a cabinet, and a built-in bar appeared. In the lower left-hand corner of the cabinet, Jenny saw an RPK machine gun. That is one big, bad Iraqi weapon. What was Amar up to?

"Wine, whiskey or beer," he asked.

"Beer will do," Jenny said.

He handed her a Corona and took one for himself.

"Kasim, would you like beer," he asked the other man.

"No, sir, thank you," he said then excused himself and left the cabin.

"Now, Jenny, tell me about yourself," Amar said as he led her to the couch and pulled her down next to him.

This wasn't Jenny's first rodeo, but she wanted to learn as much about Amar as she could. She would just have to stop him before it went too far.

"Well, I'm from New Orleans," she lied. "I moved to Michigan five years ago. I ran a hedge fund, and now I'm retired. I met Juba a month ago and saw a way to make some big money."

"Do you know what it is that he does?" Amar asked.

"Basically. He sells boats for people who are losing them anyway. Splits the insurance money with them and then sells the boats and keeps that money too."

Amar laughed. "Oh, Jenny, you are either very naive, or you are a liar."

Jenny knew there was more to it than that but didn't know how much Amar knew.

"Has he had you take anyone for a boat ride yet?"

She still didn't want to tip her hand.

"How do you mean?"

"You know what I mean. A one-way trip for a man who doesn't really want to give up his boat," Amar said, staring into Jenny's eyes for any tell-tell sign.

"So?"

Amar laughed again.

"Jenny, you are very interesting. Juba is my partner. I don't need to know all of the details, as long as I get my money and supplies. You, my lady, may prove to be a real asset to our cause."

"Perhaps," Jenny said and tipped her beer. "But if I'm going to be helpful, I need to know what our cause is."

"In good time, Jenny. In good time."

Amar rose and reached for Jenny's hand. She gave it to him, and he pulled her up.

"Now, my Jenny, I have some details to attend to. I hope we meet again soon," and he kissed her hand.

149

"Nice to meet you, Amar. We will meet again soon, I'm sure."

"There she is," I said.

We watched Jenny step from the boat and walk to the Baha and step back on it.

The fifty-two foot Tiger Marine Express that she had been on started its engines and slowly backed out of the Marina.

"What do make of that?" Diane said. "Do you think she's looking at that boat to buy?"

"I don't know, but I'll try to find out tonight."

Chapter 32

Halfway home, I felt my cell phone ringing in my pocket. I stopped my bike on the side of the road and checked it. It was Susan Crane.

"Hello," I said.

"Mr. Derringer, this is Susan Crane. Are you busy? I can call back."

"No, its fine. How may I help you?"

"I heard from Bill. Thank God he is alright."

"Did he say where he's been?"

"Yes. It's embarrassing to tell you this, but it seems he has a girlfriend. He says he is sorry and knows he has made a mistake and wants to come back."

151

"Well, that is your decision to make. I'm afraid I can't help you there," I said, knowing she was lying to me.

"I'm sorry for sending you on a wild goose chase. Please send me a bill for your time, and I will be glad to pay it."

"What about the attack on you and the stolen files?" I asked.

"Bill sent that man to get the files from me. He needed them. The man wasn't supposed to hurt me. He was supposed to get them when I wasn't home."

"Okay, Susan, you give this some thought, though. Be careful."

"I will. Thanks again for your help."

"You're quite welcome. Goodbye, Susan."

"Goodbye, Cam."

I stood there by my bike, trying to figure out if Bill really did contact her or not. If he did, maybe he'd taken care of his problem. Whoever he was hiding from must have made a deal of some kind, or Bill was dead. I didn't really think Susan was the type of wife to have the wool pulled over her eyes quite so easily. Whatever their part was in this boat jacking, they were in it together.

I got back on my bike, and a horn went off right behind me. I jumped.

"Hey, Cam," I heard Jenny yell.

I turned and saw her right behind me.

"You just scared a couple of years out of my life," I said.

"Sorry, didn't mean to scare you. I just saw you standing here and thought you might be having a problem."

"No. Just stopped for a phone call. Where ya headed?"

"I was heading home to get ready for my big date. You only have an hour you know."

"Yes, I got a little tied up on some business. Where have you been?" I asked, hoping I wasn't coming off as nosy.

"Had to go to the store to get a few hors d'oeuvres for tonight. After last night, I thought we might need some nourishment."

"Good idea; and maybe we should close the window, so we don't lose any clothes."

We both laughed again.

"Okay, I'll see you in an hour," I said.

"Bye,' she said and drove away.

Chapter 33

John Trapper knocked on the door of the Peterson's summer cottage. It was a very nicely kept-up stilt home on the water.

Bill Crane answered the door in swimming trunks and a surfer t-shirt. He was holding a mixed drink in one hand and nine-millimeter Beretta in the other.

"Oh, it's you," he said.

"Who were you expecting; the FBI?" John said, slightly side-stepping, so the barrel wasn't aimed at him.

"You never know. Anyway, it isn't loaded. I was just cleaning it," he said, turning the gun so

John could see the magazine wasn't in. "Come on in."

John followed Bill through the house. The living room was very expensively done for a winter home. It had many extensive upgrades and a well-stocked bar along one wall.

Bill led him through the living room and onto the rear deck by way of a twelve-foot sliding door. The deck offered a fantastic view of the gulf.

"Have a seat," Bill said, motioning at a chair. "Want a drink?"

"No thanks. Just stopped by to see how things were."

"Really? A phone call wouldn't have done? What do you want, John?"

"I want to talk, privately, just us."

"Okay, talk."

"Just between us?"

Bill stared at John for a few seconds. Whatever he was about to say could be very dangerous for both of them.

"I won't say anything to anyone, but we have to agree on what we discuss. There is a lot at stake," Bill said, still absent-mindedly cleaning his gun.

"I know, but it is important."

"Okay," Bill said, "talk."

"I have come upon some information that I find, let's say, very disturbing."

155

"What is it?" Bill said, now sliding to the edge of his chair.

"It's Juba. He's working with the al-Qaeda. The money we're making from the boats is going to a man named Amar. He is using the money to finance weapons, and I think, ultimately, a weapon of mass destruction, to be used here in the United States."

"How did you get information like that?"

"I followed Juba yesterday. He met with Amar Mustafa on his boat. I contacted a friend in the FBI and asked if he had any information on an Amar Mustafa. He didn't want to tell me. He said there was an ongoing investigation. Finally, he told me just enough for me to figure it out. He wanted to know why I was interested. I told him I would have to get back to him."

"So have you?"

"No. I wanted to talk to you first. We didn't sign up for anything like this."

Bill thought for a minute. "Do you really believe Juba would be aiding the al Qaeda after what he's been through?"

"I didn't think so at first, but after some thought, it makes sense."

Bill picked up the barrel of his nine-millimeter and slid it back into place. "I don't think so. He's a strong man. I just can't believe it."

"Well, I do," John said. "I think I can work with my friend and keep you and me out of it if I prove to them that Juba is threatening our country."

Bill picked up his cloth, wiped the gun down and inspected the chamber. He slid the magazine in and worked the slide. "How are you going to prove that without getting yourself killed in the process?"

"I'll wear a wire. Maybe a small camera. I don't know, but I do know it's something that needs to be done."

Bill screwed a silencer onto the barrel of the gun. "You would really jeopardize all the money we have made, and take a chance of going to prison for all the lives that have been lost?"

"I don't think you, and I will go down for it if we help them."

Bill thought about it for a moment. This guy was a loose cannon.

Bill pointed the gun at John's head and pulled the trigger.

John stared blankly at Bill in disbelief and then fell forward, his head hitting the table.

Bill sat John backup and balanced him in his seat. He knew he couldn't move John by himself. The man had to weigh three hundred pounds. He called Juba.

Chapter 34

I knocked on Jenny's door at seven o'clock.

She answered, dressed in an oversized tie-dyed t-shirt, and as far as I could tell, nothing else.

"You look lovely as always," I said.

"As do you," she said, kissing me softly and pulling me through the door.

She had the table set with a tray of cheese and bread. A bottle of wine was already opened and breathing next to the tray.

"Wine?" she asked.

"Of course."

She poured us each a glass, handed them both to me and picked up the tray.

"How about the back porch?" she said.

"Sounds good to me. It's a beautiful night."

We walked through the house to the back porch. The screen door pushed out so I was able to use my hip and open the door for her.

A glass table sat in the center of the porch, surrounded by four cushioned chairs.

I sat the wine on the table, took the tray from her and set it down.

The back yard was very private, bordered by a wide variety of Cooper plants, Snow On The Mountain, Crotons, and Oleanders which are poisonous but pretty. Just like Jenny, I thought. In the center of the yard was a beautiful large Banyan tree. A water feature was trickling on the corner of the porch, drowning out any traffic or other outside noise.

"Beautiful," I said.

"Yes, it is. This is what sold me on the house," she said, a hint of pride in her voice.

I picked up my wine glass and held it out. She raised her glass, and we clicked them in a toast. "To all of the beauty that surrounds me," I said, and we drank.

I took a piece of cheese, put it on a little square of bread and popped it in my mouth.

"Reblochon," I said.

"Very good," she said, smiling. "It's one of my favorites, from the Alps. I couldn't believe it when I found it today."

"Benzzies?" I said.

"Yes, they have a lot of different finger foods. I'm going to have to go back when I have more time."

We drank our wine and ate some more cheese and bread.

"I'm glad we're both eating the cheese. It is quite strong," she said.

"I'm only eating it in self-defense. I want to be able to kiss you later."

We laughed and looked out into the yard. Birds were busy doing whatever it was they did, one of them singing to his mate or prospective mate somewhere. A rooster then stuck his head through the bushes and looked around. When he thought the coast was clear, he entered the yard and let out a big **"Cock-A-Doodle-Dooooo."**

"That's a little rude when we're sitting here enjoying the serenity," Jenny said.

"Yeah, sometimes it is but they are sacred here; to some people anyway. Others would like to round them all up and have a big chicken fry."

"What about you?" she asked.

"Naw, I buy my chicken already fried."

"Yeah, I guess they're not so bad."

We sat in silence for a while, sipping wine and nibbling on cheese. I was wondering what Jenny was doing on that boat today and how I was going to find out.

"I guess I'll be leaving tomorrow. I have a flight at one- thirty," I said, breaking the silence.

"Would you like me to take you to the airport?"

"That won't be necessary. Diane is taking me. Which reminds me; she said she saw you on the docks earlier this evening," I said, sliding the fact in.

Jenny stared at me for a few seconds. I could tell she was caught off-guard, trying to decide what to say.

"Yes, I went to look at a boat a friend told me about. No luck, though. Not what I was looking for."

"Well, you'll find one. How about the one your agent is negotiating?"

"No word yet," she said and changed the subject.

"If it's your last night, we shouldn't eat and drink all our time away," she said, standing and pulling the t-shirt off over her head.

I was right. Nothing else.

I looked around.

"It's completely private here," she said.

I removed my clothes.

Chapter 35

The next morning, I busied myself packing my bags and making last-minute arrangements. Stacy and Barbie were going to keep an eye on my houseboat. Diane would also stop by and check on it.

I had reservations about leaving. It seemed I'd learned more on the boat jacking case in the last month than in the last five years.

Jack was still missing, although I really didn't expect ever to see him again, I would have loved to find the man who'd killed him, though.

Then there was Jenny. I loved spending time with her, but I couldn't help but think she was involved in all of this in some way.

The Cranes, they were a real mystery. I knew Bill was involved in the boat-insurance scam. Susan, I wasn't sure of, but I thought she knew a lot more than she put on.

John Trapper was hiding something also.

How big was this thing? Who were the Iraqi men and how did they figure in all of this?

I was writing all of these questions down when I heard Sheriff Buck call my name.

I walked out to the patio and saw him standing on the dock.

"Willie, what brings you down here again? Did you find my twenty bucks?"

"No, we have an all-points bulletin out on that one still," he said, sarcastically.

"I hear you're leaving us," he said.

"How did you hear that?"

"Good news travels fast."

"Well, you heard right. I'm going to New York. I was going to call you today and tell you so you could check on my boat once in a while."

"I'll be glad to. How long will you be gone?"

"Probably no more than a month the first trip, but if things work out, it could be at least a year."

"Well, good luck. I hope things go well for you."

"Thanks."

I stared at him for a moment. "Well?" I said.

"Well, what?"

"Why did you really come down here?"

He looked at me innocently then gave in.

"The files. I would still like to see your files on the boat jacking cases."

"I told you, they're gone," I said, raising my hands and holding them out.

"I know you told me that, but I would still like to see them. I need all the help I can get on the case. I keep running into dead ends."

Maybe he was right. Maybe I'd been trying to do too much on my own. He might see something I'd overlooked.

"I tell you what," I said. "I'll trade you. Mine for yours."

"Deal," he said. "If we work together, we find them, and we might find out what happened to Malinda."

"I'll have them here at nine-thirty," I said.

"Okay, I'll be back with mine. Thanks, Cam. Maybe we can get something done now."

"I hope so."

I called Diane and told her to bring the files when she came to pick me up.

"Are you sure you want to do that?" she said. "He could blow everything you've been working on."

"It can't get much worse. Besides, I'm going to be gone. Nothing would be getting done."

"Okay, I'll see you around nine."

Chapter 36

Billie Daryl pushed the body over the side of the boat. "So long, fatso," he said.

"How many bodies are down there now?" Crane asked.

"Lots, maybe fifteen," Billie Daryl said.

"Shit. Who would have thought it would get to this point?"

"Yeah, I'm sure the sharks have eat'n most of them by now. I know I wouldn't want to go down there."

"How are you going to explain John missing?"

"I'm not. No one knows he was with me."

Billie Daryl looked over the edge of the boat and said, "I wonder if Ronnie is still down there. Juba said that bitch shot him and threw him in, like garbage."

"Don't you think he had it coming?" Crane said.

"No! No one deserves that for just trying to get a little pussy."

The FBI boat, sitting anchored three miles away, watched Billie Daryl start the boat and turn back for Key West.

"There goes another one overboard," Agent Wootton said, lowering his binoculars. "Let's go get him."

"Can't we bust these guys, sir?" Sargent Biggs asked.

"We will, but we have bigger fish to fry first. Our nation's security is more important than a bunch of hoods killing each other."

Chapter 37

Diane arrived at nine with the files. I looked them over and removed a few items I didn't want Buck to see. I added some notes I had made regarding Jack and the Iraqi men. I ran a copy of everything and tucked mine away in my suitcase.

"I'm going to miss you, Diane," I said.

"I'm going to see you next week when I come to help you fix up your new place."

"I know, but it will only be for a short time. Just knowing you'll be leaving again makes me miss you."

"Can't get along without me, can you?"

"Can, just don't want to," I said and hugged her.

167

She held me tight. "Guess I'll miss you too."

"Can I have a hug too," Sheriff Buck said.

"Didn't hear you coming," I said, turning to see him standing on the dock again.

"Part Indian. Here're my files," he said, holding them out to me.

"Come on board, Willie. We were just about to have a drink."

Sheriff Buck looked at his watch. "A drink?"

He looked at Diane and then back at me. "What the hell," he said and stepped over the rail. "Line 'em up."

We sat at the table on the patio and sipped on Wild Turkey.

"Anything else you can tell me that's not in your files?" Buck asked.

"It would only be speculation. One thing, though, I would like for you to check on is Dave the bartender, down at Schooners. He's been missing for about four days. He was holding the chip with the pictures you'll find in the file. I went back to see if he could I.D. someone but he was gone."

"Who did you want him to I.D.?"

"Some Iraqi men," I lied. I had removed the picture of Jenny from the files. I didn't want to involve her yet.

168

"Iraqi men? You think they are involved in all this?"

"Yeah, I don't know how, but I think they are."

"I'll keep that in mind. The FBI might end up getting involved in this deeper than they already are."

The sheriff finished his drink and stood. "And my files?" he said.

I nodded at Diane. She went inside and returned with them.

"Let's get these guys," Buck said.

"We will. I'm sure of it," I said.

Buck shook my hand. "It's not going to be the same around here without you. I might even get a day off to go fishing."

He turned to Diane. She extended her hand. "Thanks for your help," she said.

"I'm only doing my job," he said. "You two are a thorn in these guy's sides. Don't push them too far. It looks like they don't mind killing."

After the sheriff left, Diane said, "He always seems friendly, but I don't trust him."

"I don't either," I said. "But maybe it's just his way. We've never had any problem with him. He has a big job."

"I guess," Diane said, and turned to watch him walk through the gate and out to the parking lot. He was a big man, she thought, and I bet he could be a mean one too.

Chapter 38

My plane touched down at JFK airport at two ten. I stayed on board until most of the passengers had deplaned. As I walked through the door, a stewardess who had been waiting on me handed me a piece of paper. "Call me," she said and smiled.

I nodded my head at her and moved on. I already loved New York.

"CAM," I heard Chad yell.

I turned to see him standing by the baggage area. He was dressed in a very expensive looking blue suit with a red tie. He had long black hair combed straight back. He looked as though he had been working out with a trainer every day. I thought about the shorts and t-shirt I was wearing and suddenly became very self-conscious.

"Cam, you look great. All tan and fit," he said and hugged me.

"You look pretty damn good yourself. I guess the easy life agrees with you," I joked.

"Pretty much. Let's get your bags."

We stood by the conveyer and waited for them to come by.

"Those two," I said, pointing at the two most worn bags on the conveyer.

Chad pointed at them, and a man reached down, pulled them off and placed them on a cart.

"This way," Chad said to both of us.

The man followed us to the exit. As we stepped through the door, a long black Lincoln pulled up to the curb, and the trunk popped open. The man placed the bags in and closed it. I reached for my wallet, to tip him. Chad said, "That's not necessary, Cam. He's with us."

"Oh," I said and stuck my hand out. "I'm Cam Derringer."

"Nice to meet you, Cam, I'm Larry Carroll," he said.

Larry opened the door for us to get in and closed it behind us. He then got in the front seat with the driver.

"How was your flight?" Chad asked.

"Smooth. I had wonderful service and then got the stewardess's phone number."

"Some things never change," he said.

We talked about old times and old friends as we rode through the city and into Manhattan. We turned into the parking garage for the Waldorf Astoria Hotel.

"Do we have business here?" I said, looking down at my clothes. "I'm not exactly dressed for this."

"No. No business. This is where you'll be living until you find an apartment."

"Jesus, I'd forgotten what it was like to have money, but really, Chad, I can't afford this. Not yet."

"The firm is paying," he said. "Just enjoy."

"Okay, if you insist. I will," and laughed.

I had stayed here before, back when I had money and could stay anywhere I wanted to. Now, though, after living in Key West for all these years, I had forgotten how the other half lived.

We checked into the room, and Chad and Larry came up with me. The room was exquisite. A bottle of Wild Turkey sat on the center table next to a full ice bucket. A table along the wall held an assortment of appetizers.

Chad took off his jacket and loosened his tie.

"Ready to unwind a little?" he said.

"Oh yeah," I replied. "I'm ready. You'll join us won't you, Larry."

"Just water for me," he said. "Stomach thing, you know."

We ate and drank and regressed a little to our college days.

Around six o'clock, Chad said, "Take a shower and change clothes. I'll be back in one hour to get you. We'll go eat and then to a night club."

"Okay, Chad, I know we have some lost time to make up for, but how about we just go eat tonight and maybe do the club tomorrow night. It's been a long day for me."

"You're right, Cam. I get a little carried away sometimes. I'll see you in an hour."

"Sounds good."

When Chad and Larry left, I called Diane.

"Wish you were here," I told her.

"No, you don't. I bet you're staying in some first-class hotel and drinking champagne," she said.

"Wild Turkey," I said.

Chapter 39

Amar Mustafa walked out of what appeared to be an abandoned warehouse along Miami's Little West River.

A man waited for him in a black Jaguar. Amar got in, and they drove away.

"How did it go?" Kasim asked him.

"Not good, now he says he needs seven hundred thousand for the Bomb."

"Can we get it?"

"We can get it, but it won't be easy. We need it in one week. After I do get it, I will kill all of these men. They lied to me. I will pay them, but I will kill them," Amar repeated.

Amar called Juba on their private cell phones.

"Yes," Juba answered.

"We have to talk," Amar said.

"Same place tomorrow morning at ten o'clock."

"No, I'm flying back from Miami. I'll be there at eight-thirty."

"We can't meet there at eight-thirty. It wouldn't be safe."

"Let's meet at your house at nine."

"Too dangerous."

"Meet me at the shipyard, dock two where we met before," Amar said.

"Okay, be careful you're not followed."

They hung up, and Juba called Billie Daryl and instructed him to hide in the storage building at the dock. "Take a rifle. If Amar so much as acts like he's going to attack me, shoot him."

"Will do," Billie said.

The docks were abandoned in the evening except for a few small fishing boats. On one side, seven were rocking slightly from the waves created by a passing pleasure craft.

An old freightliner, long-neglected, blocked the other side. It's rusty hull and bent railing holding perfectly still like it might actually be sitting on the bottom.

Juba pulled into the lot and parked. He got out of his car and walked toward two men who looked as though they were fishing from the end of the dock.

"Catch anything?" Juba said.

Amar turned and smiled, "Not today my friend."

"What's so important to take a chance of being spotted together?"

"We need another three hundred thousand in one week to get the bomb."

"Are you crazy?"

"Some may think so, but not you, Juba. I know you understand more than anyone how important it is to carry out this mission for Allah."

"Even so, how are we going to get the money so quickly?"

"I trust you to find a way," Amar said.

Juba turned to leave just as the pleasure craft was docking. The couple aboard it were in the dark, but the girl looked up in time to see Juba getting into his car.

I wonder what he's doing here, Diane thought. She looked around the dock and saw the two men at the other end. They appeared to be fishing, but they weren't really dressed for it and didn't have a cooler.

She hugged her date and kissed him softly. "Let's have a drink before we leave, okay?" she said.

"Sure," he said.

While he was fixing the drinks, Diane moved to the other end of the boat to get a better look at the men.

They turned to leave when they were sure Juba had gone.

Diane could see their faces now. They were the Iraqis from the boat.

"That's strange," she said to herself.

After Amar had left, Billie Daryl stepped from the storage shed. He held his rifle down at his side.

He looked around to be sure no one would see him before he stepped out into the open.

He saw a couple on a small pleasure craft across the dock. The girl was watching the Jaguar leave. He stepped back into the shadow and aimed his rifle at the girl in order to see her more clearly through the scope.

I know her. That's Diane, Cam's assistant, he thought to himself. I wonder how much she saw.

Chapter 40

I met Chad in his office the next morning.

"Good morning, Cam," he said. "How's the head this morning?"

"I've been better. Remind me to never go to supper with you if I can't stay out until one A.M.."

"I tried to get you to go home, but you kept insisting we have one more."

"Really, I don't remember that."

"Anyway, let me show you around the shop," Chad said, opening the door and standing back for me to go first.

Larry was waiting outside the office.

"Cam, Larry will be available to help you settle in. If you need to go anywhere, just let him know."

I shook Larry's hand. "Thank you, Larry. It's nice of you to help."

"If you need anything, just let me know," he said.

"I will."

We continued to tour the offices. Larry came with us.

"The space is quite impressive," I said.

His offices were very tastefully decorated and spacious. Five of them had fantastic views of Manhattan.

"This is your office," Chad said as we entered one of the rooms with the view.

"Are you sure?" I asked him.

"I told you-you were going to like it here."

"I think you were right."

I walked to the big window facing down Broadway. I could see Battery Park.

"Beautiful," I said.

"Yes, it is," Chad said.

There was an oversized cherry desk with its back to the window. A pair of cushioned chairs sat on either side, offering the lucky occupants a beautiful view of Manhattan.

"Shall we see the rest of the building?" Chad said.

"Lead the way."

We ended up back at Chad's office. Larry was with us every step of the way. I wondered what his job was. It seemed to me he didn't want Chad and me to be alone.

"Okay, Cam, that's the grand tour. What do you think?"

"I think you have done very well for yourself. You must be very proud."

"I am, thank you. And you will be doing very well for yourself also."

"I hope to," I said.

It was Thursday. Chad told me to take off until Monday morning and search for an apartment. He handed me a list. "These are some prospective apartments. My assistant scouted them for you. You might want to look at these first."

I took the list and glanced at it. They were all in the downtown Manhattan area—a very expensive area.

"You get a ten thousand dollar a month budget for living expenses," Chad said.

"Thank's again," I said.

"You are welcome. Thank you for coming. I know I'm the one coming out ahead on this deal.

Chapter 41

Juba sat at his desk in his private home office. Amar needed three hundred thousand dollars to complete the mission. The money wasn't a problem. Juba had that much in his safe. The problem was that the supplier was holding the bomb ransom from them. Juba didn't need anyone who wasn't loyal to the cause walking around and maybe telling someone he was involved.

And now, according to Billie Daryl, Diane might be piecing things together.

Juba called Jenny. "Can you come over tonight around five?"

"Not a problem. What do you need?"

"I'll tell you when you get here."

"Okay, I'll see you at five."

When they hung up, he called Amar.

"Juba," Amar said, "that was fast. I hope you have good news."

"I do. Jenny will bring the money to you at six."

"Fine, I knew you could be counted on."

"I would like to know the names and location of the men holding the bomb. I don't like to be taken advantage of."

"I will take care of these men and bring the money back to you."

"Thank you," Juba said.

~*~

Jenny rode her bicycle down to the docks where she had met with Amar. The dock security house door was standing open and she could see a man inside.

Jenny walked to the door and knocked lightly. "Hello," she said, softly.

The man turned around, and seeing Jenny, smiled. "Hello, what can I do for you?"

Jenny stuck out her hand and smiled her best smile. "I'm Jenny Jacobs."

"I'm Dan Haden," he said and shook her hand.

"I've been looking at boats for sale and wondered if you could tell me a little about one that is docked here?"

"Sure, if I can."

They stepped out of the building and onto the dock. Jenny pointed at Amar's boat. "That fifty-two-foot Tiger."

"I didn't realize it was for sale."

"Yes, I looked at it a few days ago."

"Well, I can't really tell you much about it except that it is owned by an aircraft restore company in Chicago. There are two Iraqi men here on business who checked in with me last week."

"Do they seem to be legitimate?"

"They do to me. They haven't caused any trouble and are current on their fees. How did you know the boat was for sale?"

"My broker told me," Jenny said. "Well, thanks for the info," and shook Dan's hand again.

"You're welcome. Sorry I couldn't be more help."

"You were plenty of help," Jenny said as she turned and walked away.

Jenny walked back to her bicycle, satisfied that if anyone asked about the boat now, Dan would tell him or her it was for sale. Her cover to Cam would be safe.

Chapter 42

Sheriff Buck called me early Friday evening in New York.

"How's the big city treating you?" he asked.

"Actually, not bad. How are things there?"

"I checked things out down at the docks today. There was a fifty-two-foot Tiger in the slip you were questioning in your files. I asked the dockmaster and it seems there are two Iraqi men on board. Supposedly, they are here on business and are trying to sell their company boat while they're at it. I met with them, and they seem legit," Buck said.

"Good, you don't know how glad I am to hear that," I said, thinking now that Jenny was being level with me about her business with them.

"Have you moved into an apartment yet?" Buck asked.

"No, still looking. Diane is supposed to be here in two days. She'll help me get settled."

"I don't doubt that. She doesn't let any grass grow under her feet."

"Yeah, I know. You have anything else yet?"

"No. I'll call you when and if I hear anything."

"Thanks for the update."

"That's okay. Good luck."

"Thanks."

Sheriff Buck hung up and felt satisfied with his talk with Cam.

He heard a knock at his door.

He looked at his old German wall clock that always ran three minutes slow. Four fifty-seven.

He opened the door. "Jenny, right on time."

"Hello Juba," Jenny said.

Chapter 43

"Come on in, Jenny," Buck said. "Can I get you a drink?"

"Don't mind if I do."

"I just hung up from Cam. He's doing fine. Still looking for an apartment," Buck said while filling two glasses with ice.

"Does he suspect anything?

"No, I don't think so. It's lucky for him that job offer came through for New York, though. I was afraid we were going to have to take him for a boat ride. I would have hated that."

"Me too," Jenny said. "I spent a lot of time with him to make sure we knew what he knew. I kind of got to like the old boy."

"Diane saw me meeting with Amar the other night. I told Cam I met with them to check out their story."

"Good thinking. What is their story?"

Buck looked at Jenny while pouring the Knob Creek into their glasses.

"Need to know basis," he said, sternly.

'I think I need to know," Jenny replied, equally as sternly. "If I'm going to keep meeting with him and doing business, I would like to know what kind of man I'm dealing with."

Buck brought the two glasses to where Jenny was sitting on the sofa. He sat them on the table and took a seat next to her.

"Okay, I'll tell you. You're dealing with a very dangerous man. Never let down your guard around him. You could die."

"What are we doing, Juba? What is all the money for?"

"Are you sure you want to know the details? Life would be much simpler if you knew nothing."

"It doesn't really matter to me what the money goes for as long as I get my cut. I have already killed some men for you."

Buck picked up his drink and took a long sip. He held it in his mouth and stared at the floor, then swallowed and sat the glass back down on the table.

"Very well, I will tell you a story first, then you decide if our cause is just."

Jenny picked up her drink and sat back on the sofa. She knew the next few moments would change her position in this game.

Buck began.

"I was in the Marine Corps in Afghanistan and Iraq. My special skill was that I could pick a fly off your nose at twelve hundred yards with my m110. The Iraqi word for sniper is 'Juba'."

Buck took a big swallow of his drink.

"I befriended an Iraqi family in Bagdad while I was there. A lot of soldiers did. They were people just like us, just different beliefs. They were good, kind people. They had a son, fifteen, and a daughter, twenty, Farrah. She was very pretty. I kind of developed a thing for her," Buck said, looking to Jenny for understanding.

"Nothing ever happened but I had plans to marry her and bring her back here with me. I told her father one day. To my surprise he was elated."

"One day I was sent out on a mission to eliminate a team of Jubas, twenty miles north of Bagdad. There were four of us, and we were going

189

to be gone for at least a week. We had done this before and were good at it."

Buck picked up his drink and took a long sip. He held it in his mouth and stared at the glass as if he were looking for answers to his sadness.

"Things went wrong this time. We were spotted, and before we knew what happened, we were right in the middle of a mortar attack. I watched two of my good friends fly through the air and disappear. That left Ted Trueblood and me."

"Ted was twenty-two and as mean as they come. He wasn't afraid of anything or anyone. In my opinion, that was just stupidity."

"He slid over to the right and out of sight. I went left. The mortars kept coming. It was deafening. The next thing I knew, two of the mortar launchers were silenced. Ted had taken them out. I took aim and silenced a third. Then Ted jumped up and rushed the final position. He dove right into their bunker and walked out a minute later with the launcher. I couldn't believe his nerve."

Buck raised his glass and downed the rest of his drink.

"Another?" he said, looking at Jenny.

Jenny looked down at her drink and realized she hadn't touched it. She raised it to her lips and drank it all. "Yes, I think I will."

Buck mixed the drinks, picked up a bowl of nuts and brought them back to the table.

Without touching either, he continued. "I met Ted halfway back from the bunker. I raised my hand to high five him, and he hit me in the jaw. I thought he'd broken it. I was down and didn't know if I was going to get back up. He said, 'You son of a bitch. There were no mortar bunkers out here when we scouted yesterday. Did you say anything to Farrah about our mission?' I told him I didn't say a word. He didn't believe me, but it was true, I hadn't."

"Ted had made his feelings clear to me in the past about how he felt about me being friends with the family. He said we should just kill them all and let God sort out the good ones."

Buck picked a nut from the bowl, ate it and took a big drink. Jenny took the opportunity to sip hers.

Buck looked at his watch. "Anyway, to make a long story short, a week later, Amar's son was found dead. Shot in the head at close range. The next day, Farrah was found in their house. She had repeatedly been raped and her throat cut. My first thought was Ted. When I confronted him about it, he just laughed, looked up and said, 'There you go, God, two more.' This time it was my turn to hit him, and I did. Then I reported my beliefs to Commander Bosse. He said, 'Let it go, son.

Sometimes things have a way of taking care of themselves.' I knew the son of a bitch put a hit on them. Ted must have told him he thought they were informants for the al-Qaeda."

"Do you think they were?" Jenny asked.

"Of course not. They hated the al-Qaeda. They wanted peace for their country."

"But aren't they working with the al-Qaeda now?"

"Why would you think that?" Buck said, now looking at Jenny with suspicion in his eyes.

Jenny took a drink of her whiskey and said, "Well, Amar, he looks like he could be al-Qaeda with all the money he's getting. Why else would you be giving him all that money?"

"Not just for the al-Qaeda," Buck said, disgust in his voice.

"Sorry, I didn't mean anything by that. It's just the way it looks to me."

"Well, you're wrong. The money is for us also. I've been working on this for six years. I worked my way into the boat-jacking business and drug trade. Bill already had a good thing going. I discovered he was committing insurance fraud. Told him I wouldn't bust him if I could get in on it. It was a win-win situation you might say."

"And the money?" Jenny pushed.

Buck turned again and looked into her eyes. "A bomb."

Jenny tried to hide the shock in them but couldn't.

Buck smiled, "I told you-you didn't want to know."

"What's the bomb for?"

"Ted."

"Ted?"

"Yes. He and the Commander are stationed at Quantico, Virginia, and the rest of the squad will all be there in one tidy little group. We've been waiting for all of them to be together. In three weeks they will be. It's an all-time reunion. They even invited me. I'll be there," he said, smiling across the room as if someone was standing there. "I'll be there."

"And the bomb?"

"It will be coming down the Potomac River. Amar will be bringing it. It will be in a supply shipment. I'll have a transport to bring it to our reunion as a gift. They'll get a bang out of it when I hit the button," Buck said and laughed loudly. He sounded like a lunatic.

"We're hiding it in the food truck with the caterers."

"It's all for revenge?" Jenny said.

"Pretty much. But also for the al-Qaeda. It benefits us both. "You see, after Farrah was murdered, I hated the United States and all it stood for. I made arrangements to meet with some high-ranking al-Qaeda members. I fed them some information that resulted in the deaths of some of the men I felt were responsible for Farrah's death. Eventually, I could see their side of the war. They were only protecting their land and beliefs. I agreed to work with them, still am."

"So the bomb is large enough to kill the Commander, Ted and some of the men?" Jenny said.

"No," Buck chuckled, "it will destroy the whole base. Now, Jenny, it's time for you to deliver the money."

Chapter 44

I met Diane at the baggage pick-up at JFK on Sunday morning. She looked wonderful in her faded blue jeans and Rum City Bar t-shirt, hanging off her right shoulder.

I opened my arms, and she stepped in. I already missed her. How was I going to be able to stay here for a year?

"Hello, Cam. Get mugged yet?" she asked.

"Only once; I would have gotten away, but she was too fast."

We collected her small suitcase and went to the waiting limo. Larry opened the door for us, and we settled in the back seat.

"My personal servant," I said loud enough for Larry to hear.

He got in the front seat with the driver again.

Larry turned in his seat and gave Diane a little wave. She waved back.

"That's Larry Carroll," I said. "He's helping me find an apartment."

"Any luck yet?"

"Not yet, but I know you'll find me one soon enough," I said.

"I'll try."

"How are things back in the real world?"

"Warm, muggy, loud, drunk. Same o, same o."

"Ah, I miss it already."

"One thing kind of bothers me, though."

"What's that?"

"I saw Sheriff Buck talking to those Iraqi guys the other night, down at the old Marina."

"Yes, he told me he met with them, and everything seemed to check out."

"It just seemed kind of secretive to meet them there so late."

"You think something's not right?" I'd learned to trust her intuition.

"I don't know. It just didn't feel right."

"Does he know you saw him?"

"No, I don't think so."

I thought back to our conversation. I didn't think he would have told me he'd met with them if he had something to hide.

"Just be careful around him until we get things figured out," I told her.

"I will."

Larry listened intently to their conversation and made some notes in his notebook.

We arrived at the Waldorf and told Larry we could handle her small bag from here.

"I will pick the two of you up tomorrow around ten and show you some more apartments," Larry said.

"That will be fine," I told him, "but I think Chad wants me to check in with him tomorrow at the office."

"We'll do that too," he said.

Diane was more than impressed with our suite at the Waldorf.

"Well, aren't you special," she said.

"I think so."

"You have anything to drink here?"

"Wild Turkey, coke, orange juice and milk."

"Perfect. Milk will do."

Diane opened her suitcase and produced a white sack.

"Is that what I think it is?" I asked.

"If you think it's chocolate honey-buns, it is. It's Sunday morning isn't it?"

"I'll get the milk."

Chapter 45

Diane and I were having breakfast at the Oscar's Brasserie in the Waldorf. It was a very richly appointed dining room. The breakfast buffet was fantastic.

Diane wore a red blouse and a very short black skirt. Silver stiletto heels showed off her perfect runner's legs. I had on my best suit, glad to see it still fit, and a red tie. We looked good together if I do say so myself.

We had just finished our meal and were enjoying a cup of coffee when Larry walked in. He looked around, and I held my hand up. He saw me and came to our table.

"Have a seat," I said, pointing at a chair.

"Thank you," he said and sat down.

"Hello, Diane. You look lovely this morning," he said.

"Thank you. I don't get to dress up much anymore. Not much call for it in Key West."

"Do you have a plan for the day?" I asked.

"First of all, I talked to Chad. He said he didn't know what he was thinking, asking you to come to the office today. You're a free man. We can look at some apartments and have lunch. If you decide on one, we'll go back and write a contract."

"Great," Diane said.

"Yes, maybe we'll get it over with today," I said.

Larry ordered coffee, and we chatted while we finished.

Larry said he had worked for Chad for two years. "I'm not an attorney," he said. "I just do odd jobs. I'm a retired cop."

"Odd jobs like this one?" I asked.

"No, this is my first apartment hunting job, and I hope my last. Although the company I'm keeping today is much more lovely than the last two days," he said, looking at Diane.

"You don't look old enough to be retired," I said, thinking he was maybe forty. He was a little overweight and looked a lot like Colonel Sanders, premature white goatee and all.

"I took a bullet. Early retirement."

We sat in silence while I signed the check, charging it to my room.

"Are you ready?" I asked.

"Let's do it," he said.

When we walked out the front door, the limo drew up, and Larry opened the back door for us and climbed into the front with the driver again.

"Wouldn't you be more comfortable back here?" I asked. "That way we can talk over the prospective apartments."

"Naw, I' m good. If you see one you like, then we'll go over it."

We rode for about three blocks before coming to the first one. Larry opened our door and said, "608. The realtor is waiting for you there. I'll just wait here if you don't mind."

"That's fine Larry. We'll see you in a few," I said.

I saw him watching Diane as she walked to the front door. The apartments were housed in an old, ornate building by today's standards. The front door was a ten-foot-tall wooden masterpiece. The leaded glass was original but looked as good as the day it was installed.

As we approached it, the door opened, and a uniformed door attendant stepped aside, tipped his hat to Diane and said, "Welcome, Mr. Derringer."

"Thank you," I said.

"The elevator is on the right, just past the lobby."

I thanked him again, put my hand on the small of Diane's back and steered her toward the elevator.

"Aren't you the gentleman," she said.

"I'm afraid someone is going to steal you before you can find me an apartment."

The elevator was black marble trimmed in brass. It stopped on the sixth floor and opened silently. The hallway was richly carpeted and about twelve feet wide. There were tables with lamps and winged back chairs along the walls.

608 was halfway down the hall, on the right. We started to knock when the door opened.

An attractive lady in her mid-thirties smiled at us and said, "Welcome home, Mr. Derringer." She then stuck out her hand to Diane and said, "Hello, Diane, I'm Kim West."

"Nice to meet you, Kim," we said in unison and laughed.

Kim held the door open for us as we entered. She looked down the hall in both directions then stepped in and closed the door.

I looked at her because that seemed a little suspicious. She held her finger to her lips to shush me and handed me a note.

While I was reading it, she showed Diane around the apartment. They were talking normally about the rooms and the building.

Diane got it that she was supposed to act normal.

The note was from Chad.

Cam, you can trust Kim if you want to send a note back to me. She's a long-time friend of our family.

First of all, our deal to get your license back is real. Nothing can change that. With that being said, Larry is with the FBI. He and his partner were in my office when I called you. Our phones are tapped as well as your hotel room and my office.

They wanted you here because you were getting too close to finding out who was behind the boat thefts. They are working on a bigger case and the two are related. For your safety and Diane's, I hope you decide to stay here and let them handle this.

I wanted you to know what was going on, though, because I know how important this case is to you. I know you want to know what happened to Malinda. So do I. I'll stand beside your decision, and you will always have a job here.

Be careful.
Chad"

When I finished reading the letter, I handed it to Diane and took my turn talking to Kim about the apartment.

It was exquisite, but my heart wasn't in it now. Everything I knew about the case was going through my mind. He said I was close. Close to what, though? Was Jenny really mixed up in all of this?

I had to get back to Key West. Maybe Sheriff Buck could help me sort out the details. There must have been something I'd missed.

Chapter 46

I took the note from Diane when she'd finished it. She had a shocked look on her face and an oh-no look in her eyes. She knew what I was going to do.

I turned the note over and wrote on the back.

Thanks, Chad. I guess you know what I have to do. Maybe when this is over, I can come back and work with you. You're a good friend.

I handed the note to Kim.

"Thank you, Kim, for showing us the apartment. It is quite lovely. We will let you know of our decision tomorrow if not sooner. We have a few more to look at today before we decide."

"That will be fine. I hope you decide to make this your home. It won't be on the market long, though."

Diane hugged her, and we left.

We knew we couldn't discuss what we had just learned. Our phones would have listening devices in them and they could probably hear our conversations as well.

"What did you think about the apartment?" Diane asked.

"Very interesting."

"I thought it was beautiful. I think you should buy it and settle in," she said, squeezing my arm.

"You know I can't do that without giving the rest some thought," I said, both of us knowing what the other meant.

"Think long, think wrong," she said.

Larry was waiting by the limo. He opened the door and we stepped in.

When we were settled, he said, "Do we need to look any further or are you ready to settle in?"

I thought that was an interesting choice of words. He had clearly been listening to our conversation.

"Let's look at another first and then maybe we can decide," I said. "We don't want to make any hasty decisions."

"Very well," he said. "The next one is only two blocks from here."

We spent another hour looking at the second apartment. I didn't really take in any of the information the young man was telling us about the history of the building or the past tenants that had lived there. I did hear some famous names being thrown at me, but I couldn't have cared less.

We thanked him when we finally got the opportunity to speak and told him we would be making a decision soon.

Larry asked if we would like to get some lunch.

"I hate to do it, but I think I'm going to have to pass. My stomach is not feeling so good today. I think I've been doing too much celebrating since I arrived. I believe I'll eat something light in my room and think about the two apartments we looked at today, so I can get this behind me," I said, feigning fatigue.

"Okay, Cam, we'll drive you back, and when you make a decision, you call me and we'll take care of the details," Larry said.

"Thank you. You've been a big help."

Once back at our hotel, we went to our room. I took out my cell phone, laid it on the bed and motioned for Diane to do the same.

"Why don't we go down to the restaurant, have a light meal and then you can explore New York while I get some rest," I said.

"Sounds good to me," Dianne said.

Leaving our phones on the bed, we left the room.

"What do you think?" I asked her once we were in the elevator.

"I think we need to go over our notes again. We missed something. We're close. But if we go back they'll know Chad must have been the one to tell us."

"I think I have a plan for that. I need to use the house phone."

I approached the desk in the lobby and asked the concierge if I could use the phone.

"Yes, sir, Mister Derringer," he said and handed the phone to me.

I called Stacy.

Chapter 47

I was back in my room quietly going over my notes when my cell phone rang.

I looked at the caller I.D. It was Stacy.

"Hello," I said.

"Cam, this is Stacy. Did I catch you at a bad time?"

"No, not at all, Stacy. To what do I owe this pleasure?"

"Well, I didn't want to bother you, but I don't know who else to call."

"Is something wrong, Stacy?"

"It's Barbie. She left two days ago to go shopping, and I haven't heard from her since. She wouldn't have gone away and not told me. We share everything," she said, worry in her voice.

She was doing a good job. Just the way I had told her to do it.

"Is there anyone here that you could recommend for me to contact? I have a bad feeling about this. I wish you were here," she said and started to cry.

"Stacy, just calm down. I'll talk to Chad and see what I can do. I'll call you back. Maybe I can arrange to come back for a while."

"Oh thanks, Cam. Do you think we can find her?"

"Don't worry, Stacy. I would never let anything happen to her."

After we had hung up, I called Chad.

"Hello, Cam. Did you find an apartment?"

"Well, the first one was quite interesting, but I'm afraid I got some disturbing news a few minutes ago. It seems one of my friends in Key West has gone missing and I've been retained to find her."

"Does that mean you're going back to Key West?"

"Yes, it does. I feel I have to."

"Is there anything I can do to change your mind?"

"No, I'm afraid not, Chad. This is important. I promise I'll come back when I'm finished if that's okay."

"You're always welcome here."

"Thanks."

Chapter 48

Larry Carroll bulldozed his way into Chad's office. Chad looked up from his desk and saw the look on his face. His cheeks were red, the veins in his neck bulged and his eyes were unblinking.

Chad flashed back to his college days when his father had found his stash of marijuana in his sock drawer. When his father had confronted him, he'd looked just like Larry.

"You told him didn't you!" Larry yelled.

"No, I didn't, Larry. He doesn't know a thing. He just had to return to help a friend."

"If I find out that you told him what we were doing, I'll have your license," Larry spat and hurried out of the room.

Chad sat back in his chair and smiled. He didn't like Larry. For that matter, he didn't like the FBI. They felt they had the right to run your life the way they saw fit. Now I just hope Cam can get out of town before they find him.

I was busy packing my suitcase when Diane came in. She looked at the half-packed case and the pile of clothes on the bed next to it and then back at the case.

"Where are you going?" she asked.

"Stacy called. Barbie has been missing for two days. She's worried, and I'm going to go help find her," I said, both of us still playing the part for the listening devices they had planted.

"Let me do that. You'll never get all that in there," she said, stepping in front of me and pushing me aside.

"What do you think happened to her?"

"Don't know, but it's not like her to leave and not tell anyone."

~*~

Back in Key West, Barbie was driving up Highway 1 toward Marathon Key, to a very nice

213

resort that had been booked for her for a week. "If that's what Cam wants then I'll be more than happy to kick back and relax for a while," Barbie said aloud to herself.

Chapter 49

Billie Daryl walked into Sheriff Buck's office. He was wearing his deputy uniform, which Buck had given him to wear on special occasions when he was deputized.

"Billie," Buck said, "we have a little trouble. Bill Crane has gone missing, this time for real. Now that I think about it, I guess the last time was just a trial run for the real thing. He knows way too much, and I don't want him out there talking. He killed John for the same reason, and now I think it's his turn."

"Any idea where he might be?"

"If I had an idea where he was, I'd go get him myself. Now go find him. Start at his house. Lean on Susan if he's not there. Just find him."

Billie Daryl walked out of the sheriff's office into the bright sunshine. He stretched his arms out like a cross and yawned.

"Screw you, Buck," he said to himself, got in the squad car and turned south on Highway 1.

Billie Daryl pulled into the driveway of Bill Crane's house. The lights were out as far as he could tell. It was daylight, but the lot was shaded thanks to the large trees in the front yard.

He stepped onto the front porch and peeked into the window before knocking on the door. It looked to him like no one was home.

He knocked three times and put his ear to the door. Nothing. He went back to the window and looked in again. He could see a few boxes scattered around and some papers on the floor. Some of the furniture was out of place.

He walked around to the back door by way of a stone path that meandered through a flower garden and then under a trellis with a vine full of beautiful yellow flowers. He didn't know one from another but stopped to smell the flowers that were in full bloom. They reminded him of his childhood home where his mother would nourish and talk to her flowers. "At least she nourished something," he thought.

He stepped onto the back porch and looked in the window over the kitchen sink. Still nothing. He tried the door. It came open. Someone had left and not bothered to lock it. He stepped in.

The house was quiet, eerily quiet. It had the feel of abandonment. He checked the closets and desk drawers, all were empty. He picked up a few of the papers on the floor to see if they might hold a clue as to where the Cranes could have gone. Nothing.

"Buck's not going to like this," he thought.

Chapter 50

Diane and I arrived back in Key West at eight-thirty, Tuesday morning. The red-eye flight had taken some of the fight out of us so we decided to go to our separate homes and catch a nap before we rejoined the real world.

I hailed a taxi, dropped Diane off at her house and told the driver where I lived.

"They had some big trouble over that way last night," he said.

"At the boat dock?" I asked.

"Yeah, some fella's houseboat blew up and sank."

I had a bad feeling about this. About that time, my new cell phone I'd bought before leaving New

York rang. My number was the same, and I had the phone book downloaded. It was Diane.

"Are you home yet?" she asked, she was crying.

"Not yet. We've got a few blocks to go. What's wrong?"

"Your houseboat, it's gone. I'm watching it on the news now. It blew up last night."

My worst fear had been realized. I was now homeless, and all my possessions were gone. I immediately thought about Malinda's menagerie collection. I would have nothing of hers to hold and look at when I wanted to think about her.

My thoughts then went to the FBI.

"Cam, are you there? Are you okay?" Diane said into my ear.

"Yes, I'm here," I said weakly. The picture of tornado victims I had seen on TV went through my mind. This must have been how they had felt.

"I'll be right there, Cam," Diane said and hung up.

The taxi turned the corner and aimed toward the small marina where I once lived but now didn't. I could see yellow crime tape across the gate that led to the dock where I'd strolled many times with my friends. I could picture myself carrying my bag of groceries up the walkway to my boat. I could picture Jenny's bike leaning against the gate-post.

Wait a minute, Jenny's bike *was* leaning against the gate. I looked down the dock. Jenny was standing at Stacy's boat, talking to her.

"It looked like quite a mess on TV," the taxi driver said. "I hope it wasn't yours."

"I'm afraid it was. Did they say what happened?"

"Nope. Still investigating. Sorry man, what a bummer."

I paid the driver and gave him a generous tip.

"Thanks, man," he said. "Do you want me to hang around?"

"No thanks. I have a friend coming."

I walked to the dock in somewhat of a daze. Jenny saw me and met me at the gate.

"Cam, I'm so sorry. I saw it on the news this morning," she said and hugged me.

I automatically hugged her back, but my heart wasn't in it.

"How bad is it?" I asked, not daring to look down the dock yet.

"Well, something blew a hole in the side, and it took on water. The stern filled first and sank to the bottom. Luckily, air was trapped in the bow, and it's still above water. Everything in the front half of the boat is still dry. They're going to float the back up again with airbags."

"Who is doing all of this? Why would someone go to all the trouble to raise my boat? I didn't authorize any of this," I said, puzzled.

"Stacy said she saw a man go on board. No one left before the explosion."

"How did you know I was going to be here?"

"I didn't until I got here. Stacy told me you were coming home to help her find Barbie."

Just then, Stacy came to the gate. She hugged me, and I hugged her back. I felt I had more of a bond with her now than I had before.

"Cam, I'm so sorry. I should have called the Sheriff as soon as I saw him enter your boat, but then I thought it was the Sheriff. It was dark, though, and I couldn't see that well," Stacy said, half crying.

"Why did you think it was Buck?"

"It's just that he was a big man, but after the explosion, I called him right away. He was in his office," she said and then the gates opened, and she started sobbing uncontrollably.

I put my arms around her and comforted her. "It's okay, Stacy. There is nothing you could have done. We'll fix everything."

I looked at Jenny and nodded at Stacy, asking her to take over for me. Jenny got the message and put her arms around her. Stacy went to her, freeing me.

The dock was littered with bits of paper and wood debris I assumed were part of my boat. I stepped over and around them, not wanting to impede any investigation. I could now see my boat, the nose rising high into the air. A group of men were gathered on the dock, talking. One of them was Sheriff Buck. He turned and saw me.

"Cam," he said and reached out to shake my hand. "Thank God you weren't home."

"Yeah, thank God," I said. "What the hell happened here?"

"Don't know yet. Stacy says there is someone on board, though. We have divers coming and a team to raise the back out of the water again. It's too dangerous to enter right now until we get it stabilized."

I just stood there, dumbfounded, staring at my home. My patio table had slid against the front sliding doors, broken glass visible on the threshold, the umbrella floating upside down in the water. My chairs were nowhere to be found. My guess was they had been deep-sixed.

Reporters were beginning to re-gather at the foot of the dock. I guessed they were here for the raising of the Titanic.

Chapter 51

There was a ruckus and a swarm of reporters moving toward the parking lot, all extending their mics. Diane had arrived. Most people on the Key knew who she was.

She waved off any interviews and made her way to me. She started crying when she saw the boat. I felt as though I had to comfort everyone else and didn't have time to grieve for myself.

I hugged her and patted her on the back. "Well, now I guess I'll get that new furniture you've been hounding me about," I said, trying to lighten the mood.

She looked at me, trying to process what I'd said, "Don't think I'm ever going to let you live here again."

"It's my home, of course, I'll live here again."

"You can't, it's too dangerous," she said between sobs. "What if you would have been home."

"Let's worry about those things later. Right now we need to find out what happened and who is on board."

Four hours later, with the help of the Key West fire department and a local dive shop, the fantail of my house was starting to shine in the afternoon sun.

The hole was now visible, water pouring out of it. I surmised it was in the area of my bedroom, and as if to confirm my speculation, one of my pillows poked through and sunk to the bottom of the canal.

If I weren't such a man, and if everyone wasn't watching me, I think I would have cried.

There was a sea crane with straps circled around the back of my houseboat and blue airbags secured to the side, all now holding the boat in place. The damage didn't seem as bad as I had first thought. Of course, the interior was going to have to be redone completely. The water had surely taken a toll on what wasn't blown to smithereens from the explosion.

I could see something else floating through the giant hole now. It was most assuredly an arm. It came through, fell into the canal, floated there for a couple of seconds and then started seesawing to the bottom.

Buck yelled at one of the divers and pointed to the slowly sinking arm. The man dove into the water and came up with it in his hand. He swam to the dock and tossed it up. It landed on the wood planks with a thud.

Diane turned her head away, too late. She shrieked and buried her head in my chest.

"Why don't you go home for a while and get some rest while we finish this. I'll call you when we're through for the day," I said to her.

"Okay, I think I will. Call me as soon as you're done. You can stay at my house tonight."

"I'll do that. Thank you."

Chapter 52

Twenty hours earlier:

Amar handed the man the package and one hundred dollars.

"Place it in the back cabin, in the cabinet next to the bed," he told the man. "After you get it placed, flip the lights once and wait five minutes before leaving. I'll give you the other hundred when you get back."

He watched the man walking away with the package toward the docks.

Sheriff Buck got out of his car and walked to where Amar was sitting in his SUV.

"Get in, and we'll try this out," Amar said.

Tom Burnikel was a man down on his luck. His wife, who was having an affair, had walked out on him three days earlier, taking the three hundred dollars they had stashed for an emergency.

When the Iraqi man approached him with the offer to make some easy money, he jumped on it. It would be plenty to get drunk for a couple of days while he got over the cheating bitch.

The gate squeaked as he opened it, but he didn't care. He ambled on down the dock to the big houseboat at the end and jumped over the rail.

The sliding door was locked, so he picked up a patio chair and threw it through the glass. He reached inside, unlocked the door and entered.

Once inside, he set the package down and opened a few drawers. Nothing of any value. He saw a glass unicorn on the shelf and put it in his pocket.

He picked the package up again and walked to the rear of the boat. There was a very nice king size bed there, and as the man had said, there was a cabinet next to it. He opened it, placed the package inside and closed it.

He saw the light switch on the wall next to the door and flipped it on and off. He then lay down on the big bed and stretched out. "Man, this is nicer than my bed. I could stay here forever."

Stacy heard the gate squeak and looked out her window. A man was walking to Cam's boat. He didn't look as though he was sneaking. He looked like he belonged. She watched him disappear after he jumped the rail. He was a big man. Was that Sheriff Buck?

A few minutes later, she heard glass break and then saw a light blink.

"Okay, the bomb is small, but he said to make sure it is confined in an area so innocent people won't get killed. Are you sure this is what you want to blow up?" Amar said.

"Yep," Buck said. "I think he has the other files hidden in there somewhere. This way we can test the bomb and destroy the files, and at the same time make sure Cam has no home to return to."

"Very well," Amar said. "This is supposed to work just like the one we have for Quantico. This will be a good test for us."

Amar raised his cell phone and dialed the number. "Would you like to do the honors?" he asked Buck, holding the phone up.

"Don't mind if I do," he said, taking the phone.

Sheriff Buck pushed the green send button.

Three seconds later, Cam's boat rocked from the explosion.

Fifteen seconds after that, the nose came out of the water, and the fantail started to sink.

"Works just fine," Sheriff Buck said. "We'll pick up the real thing in three days."

Sheriff Buck's phone rang. It was forwarded to his cell from his office.

"Sheriff's office. William Buck speaking," he said.

"Sheriff, this is Stacy. Cam's boat just blew up."

Chapter 53

Special Agent Sanchez sat across the table from William Crane at the FBI office in Miami.

Two days earlier, the FBI had raided the Cranes house and seized all their records. They had watched Bill from the time he'd left, three weeks before, until the time he'd returned three days ago. They wanted to let him run free a few more days, but after seeing him dump the body of John Tripper in the ocean, they thought it time to bring him in.

They cleared his house of all records, clothes and personal items so Sheriff Buck would think he'd run.

Susan was being detained down the hall. For the time being, she was in a very lush guest suite of the FBI.

"Okay, Bill," Sanchez said, "we have footage of you dropping Mr. Trapper off four days ago, along with Billie Daryl Dunn. We retrieved John Trapper five minutes after you left. There has been quite a collection of bodies down there. Right now, we have you and Billie Daryl for all the killings. I would like to tell you that you'll spend the rest of your life in prison, but I think you'll most likely die in the gas chamber."

"I didn't kill all those men," he said, "They made me go with them to dump that body."

"Who made you?"

"I need a lawyer."

"No!" Sanchez said and beat his fist on the table.

Bill jumped back and almost fell out of his chair.

"Agent Anderson has information that you, William Buck and Amar Mustafa have plans to use a weapon of mass destruction. Is that right?"

"No. I don't know what you're talking about.

"Let me read something to you. We call this an indictment, and it has your name on it."

Sanchez opened his folder and read aloud.

"The indictment alleges that 'between July 2011 and July 2015, the suspects,' that's you, Sanchez said, pointing at Bill, were conspiring to provide 'material support and resources -- including property, services, funding, lodging, communications equipment, personnel and transportation -- knowing and intending that this support be used in preparation for and in carrying out a violation of law -- namely, a conspiracy to use a weapon of mass destruction.'.

"The indictment also alleges that the suspects were 'conspiring to use a weapon of mass destruction (explosives) against persons and property within the United States' during the same time frame.

"Does that accurately describe what you were trying to do?" Sanchez asked.

"No, I don't know anything about any bombs," Bill lied.

"Too bad. I thought maybe we could work some kind of a deal if you had some information. Bill, the FBI's number one priority is counterterrorism. We don't much give a shit about the dead bodies. The police might, though, and we might be able to help you with that if you help us. The charge of murder carries a death penalty. To be exact, the indictment is not against a particular group or religion, it is against three specific individuals who, if convicted on charges of providing materials to support terrorists and to use weapons of mass destruction, can yield fifteen years in prison for the first and life for the second. Either is better than the death penalty you're most definitely facing."

"What do you want from me?"

"Where is the bomb and when will it be delivered?"

"What makes you think there is a bomb?"

"We have agents that have been watching you guys for years. We know."

"I don't know where the bomb is. I only found out there was one last week."

"Who would know and how can we get the information?"

"There's a girl. Her name is Jenny Jacobs. She is tied upright in the middle of all this. She can tell you what you need to know."

Sanchez sighed, "Take him away and bring in Mrs. Crane."

Chapter 54

My boat was finally secured to the dock and held up by additional airbags that completely encompassed the fantail. Water was still trickling out of the four-foot hole in the starboard side. From the dockside, where we were standing, the boat looked fine. Maybe a little weathered but nothing that couldn't be fixed with a little TLC.

Finally, two State Policemen boarded the boat from the bow. They slid the broken patio table away from the door and entered through the sliding door.

In less than a minute, one of the men came back out at a run, holding his hand over his mouth. He bent over the rail and threw up three times. Sheriff

Buck stepped onto the boat and waved for his deputy, Billie Daryl, to come and escort the man from the boat.

"Pussy," he said. "Get him out of here before he contaminates the crime scene."

Buck entered the boat and the other man exited, getting on his cell phone to call in a CSI team. He then leaned into the boat and said something to Sheriff Buck who exited the cabin.

Buck yelled in the State Trooper's face. "Get the hell off this boat and don't come back. This is my crime scene."

The trooper back-peddled from the giant sheriff, tripping over the tumbled patio table and falling on the broken glass.

Sheriff Buck looked down at him and pointed to the dock. The trooper got up and stepped off the boat, onto the dock. He pulled his phone out and made another call.

Buck waved him off in disgust. "Idiots," he said.

He looked at me and waved me forward. "Cam, I hate for you to see this, but do you mind taking a look at what's left of this guy and telling me if you know him?"

I could feel the bile rising in my throat. I swallowed hard.

"I guess I can, but I don't promise I'll fare any better than that trooper did."

"Wait here a minute," he said and stepped back inside. When he returned, he said, "Okay, I covered everything except his face. It's not in too bad shape."

Buck stepped back in. I reluctantly followed. I felt sick to my stomach as soon as I saw the interior of the boat. Everything was destroyed. It was even worse than I had imagined.

My furniture, which was in the front of the boat that I thought might be dry was soaked and mostly blown apart. The refrigerator was lying on its side next to the stove that was on its back and held in place by the propane gas line. My pictures were who knows where. Probably under all the debris.

"Over here," Buck said.

I stepped over what was left of my belongings and looked down at the bloody face of a man I had never seen before. Other than the blood, his face didn't look too bad. I then noticed that his body didn't seem long enough for a full-grown man. After staring for a moment, I realized that another blanket was covering something five feet away, a shoe protruding from beneath the blanket. The other half of the man.

No wonder the trooper got sick. At least it was covered before I entered.

"I've never seen him before," I said, turning my stare away from the bedroom and back out to the destroyed living quarters.

"I wonder what he was doing here?" Buck said, raising the blanket to take another look.

"I don't have the slightest idea."

"Did you have some kind of a bomb in here?" Buck said.

"No. Why would I have a bomb on my boat?"

"Just asking," Buck said.

I was wondering why Buck would think I might have a bomb. It then occurred to me that with all the insurance scams going around he might think I was trying to pull one, and then he asked, "Are you insured?"

"Yes, I am. Are you insinuating that I might have blown up my boat for the insurance?"

"No, not at all. I was just hoping you were, for your sake."

I started to look around for anything I might salvage when Buck stopped me.

"Sorry, Cam, you can't touch anything until our investigation is over. Why don't you go to Diane's and spend the night there and we'll meet here again tomorrow morning at eleven? I'll post a man here to guard your boat."

So I left. What else could I do? On the way out, I stopped at Stacy's boat. She was sitting on the patio.

"Sorry again, Cam," she said.

"Not your fault. Don't worry about it."

"But still…" and then she began to cry again.

I hugged her. I don't know if it was to comfort her or me, but we both felt better afterward.

Chapter 55

"Hello, Susan," Sanchez said as she was escorted into the room.

"I want a lawyer before you ask any questions," she said.

"No, you don't."

She looked at him in disbelief.

"And why not?" she snapped.

"Because you're implicated in running a large insurance scam," he hesitated for effect, "and murder."

She looked shocked. "Murder. Who was I supposed to have murdered?"

"John Trapper," Sanchez said.

"You're crazy."

"Bill and Billie Daryl did it, and since you were in the scam with the two of them, you're just as guilty."

"Bill wouldn't kill anyone," Susan snapped.

"Uh-huh," Sanchez said, smiling.

Susan looked down in acquiescence.

"What do you want to know?" she said softly.

"Where is the bomb and when are they going to use it?"

Susan looked back up in surprise. "Bomb, what bomb?"

"Don't act like you don't know."

"I don't. I thought you wanted to know about the insurance fraud, the boat thefts. I don't know anything about any bomb," she insisted.

"Sheriff Buck and a few others are planning on using a weapon of mass destruction against the United States. They are using the money from your boat insurance scams to fund it. That puts you right in the middle. You've been funding the al-Qaeda," Sanchez said, pointing at Susan accusatorily.

"You don't have any proof of this."

"But we do. We have a lot of proof, and if we don't start getting some answers, we're going to see you and Bill rot in prison until you die in the gas chamber."

Susan gulped nervously.

"If I tell you everything I know, what will you do for me?"

"Depends on what you know."

"I have records on every boat Buck stole or repossessed and some of the drug deals he made along with them."

"How did you come about obtaining that information?"

"First, what kind of deal can we make?"

"Still depends. What about the bomb?"

Susan banged her fist on the table and now yelled, "I DON'T KNOW ANYTHING ABOUT A BOMB."

Sanchez left the interrogation room feeling defeated. He called special agent Anderson in Key West.

"We have no idea as to when or where the bomb will be delivered," Sanchez said.

"We're working on it," Anderson replied.

Chapter 56

When I left Stacy, I took a taxi to the auto storage warehouse and retrieved my Mercedes. I tipped the valet and drove down to the docks. I wanted to retrace some of the moves I had made recently, to see if I could discover what I had missed.

I saw my friend and Harbor Master, Dan talking on his cell phone in his office. When he saw me coming, he said something and hung up.

"Cam, I was just talking to Diane. I'm sorry about your boat. Any idea what happened yet?"

"No. Some guy blew a hole in my boat and cut himself in half while he was at it. I've never seen him before."

"Shit," Dan said, looking at the ground. "What the hell?"

"Yeah, shit," I said.

"Well, what brings you down here? You need somewhere to live awhile? I've got room."

"Thanks anyway, I'm going to stay with Diane."

"Lucky."

"Funny, I don't feel lucky. Anyway, I just came to retrace some of my steps. Anything new with the Tiger in slip 24?"

"There has been some activity. They go out about twice a day. I never see anyone disembark, though."

"Have you seen anyone board?"

Just that lady, Jenny. She's the one who asked me if I had any information about it. She said she was thinking about buying it."

"How often does she visit?"

"Every couple of days. She always has a case when she goes on board but not when she leaves," Dan said, his mind drifting as he looked toward the boat.

"That's strange," I said.

"Yeah, that's what I thought."

"Thanks, Dan. Will you call me if you see her again?"

"You bet. Sorry again about your boat."

"Thanks again. See you later," I told him and started to leave.

"Oh, by the way," he said, "Dave's back at Schooners. Seems he got drunk and went fishing with Crazy Wanda. They were gone for a week. His wife is about to kill him."

"You don't say. It's a wonder that a week with Crazy Wanda didn't kill him," I said, laughing.

I left and drove to Diane's house with the intention of getting the picture of Jenny and taking it to Dave, to see if that was the woman he saw Jack with the night he disappeared.

I pulled into Diane's driveway and saw her sitting on the front porch swing, drinking a beer.

"That looks good," I said, pointing at the beer.

"Yeah, I needed it after seeing that arm thrown onto the dock. So, who was the guy?"

"Don't know. I've never seen him before."

Diane got up and went in the house. I took a seat on the swing. I knew she was getting me a Wild Turkey. She did.

"Here ya' go," she said and sat next to me.

"What now?" she asked.

"Well, Dave's back at Schooners. I thought I would take a picture of Jenny to him to see if she's the girl."

"Are you sure you want to know?"

"Only if I'm wrong."

"I hope you are. I like her."

"Yeah, me too."

We sat and talked for a while. I realized how tired I was. The activities of the day had finally caught up to me.

Diane woke me gently. She had already set my empty glass on the table next to the swing.

"Come on, Cam. Let's go to bed. We'll see Dave tomorrow."

"Good idea," I said sleepily.

Chapter 57

Amar eased the fifty-two foot Tiger away from the dock and turned toward the bay. The moon gave him enough light to find his way in the darkness. He looked up at the sky, illuminated by the moon, taking in the stars shining like diamonds.

"Soon, all of this will not matter," he told Kasim.

"It will matter—just not to us."

"And not to three thousand spineless soldiers."

"Yes, not to them," Kasim said.

The boat slipped into the darkness and turned north toward Miami. This was to be the Tiger's last visit to Key West.

"We will have a pleasant trip to Miami," Amar said.

"The seas are calm and the wind is soft. Allah is on our side," Kasim said.

~*~

Captain Lacy of the United States Coast Guard watched the fifty-two foot Tiger run quietly up the coast with its running lights off. This usually meant they didn't want to be spotted; probably moving something illegal, although sometimes it was just a drunk or high millionaire with a boat full of teenage girls out for a no clothes tour of the coast.

Either way, Captain Lacy thought he had better check it out. He hoped it was the latter of the two choices.

The Captain gave the order to intercept the Tiger. The Coast Guard boat turned and sped in the direction of Amar.

Kasim saw the large boat approaching on the radar screen.

"Amar," he said softly. "There is a boat approaching at three o'clock. One mile out. Probably Coast Guard."

"Get out the guns. We cannot let them destroy our mission."

Half a mile out from the Tiger, the Captain saw a boat on his starboard side moving in the same direction but also closing the gap between them.

He raised his megaphone and hit the switch after a blast from his horns.

"This is the United States Coast Guard. Turn your boat away immediately."

The boat kept coming.

"Prepare to fire a shot across the bow of the aggressor," Captain Lacy barked.

The guns were turned in the direction of the oncoming boat. It turned slightly and pulled ahead of the coast guard. Once in front, it cut its speed and idled its engines.

The Coast Guard boat cut its own speed and stopped next to the intruder. With their guns aimed on the boat, the Captain again raised his megaphone and told it to identify itself.

A man in an official US Navy uniform stepped from the bridge and held his hands in the air.

"Captain Lacy, I'm Lieutenant Utley. I have orders from the White House to intercept you if you tried to capture that boat. I'm working with the FBI and we have the boat under surveillance. You may come onboard and verify our credentials."

Captain Lacy looked at the men onboard the thirty-four foot Navy Sea Ark. "Hold up your ID."

Lieutenant Utley held his up. A bright light from the bow of the Coast Guard ship turned toward him and illuminated the whole boat and everyone on board.

"Turn off that damn light," the Lieutenant yelled. "What the hell are you doing? I told you we were performing reconnaissance."

The light died.

"Sorry, I didn't mean to …"

"Shit, I hope they didn't see us. This is a matter of national security."

"I should have been given a heads up then this would have never happened," the Captain said.

"We were working on a need to know basis. Please leave the area slowly. I hope you didn't blow our cover."

"They stopped beside another boat," Kasim said, looking at the radar screen.

"Now they have turned and are moving away."

"Very good. They weren't after us. Allah is with us."

Chapter 58

I was up early the next morning. I made bacon and eggs for Diane and myself and decorated the breakfast table with a vase of wildflowers I'd picked from her garden.

She poked her head in the kitchen just as the coffee finished perking. "Oh, it's you. I smelled the bacon and thought someone had broken into the house and fixed breakfast."

"I knew you'd be hungry. We didn't eat last night."

"Wow," she said, noticing the flowers. "What's the occasion?"

"I've decided to not let life get me down. My boat is insured, and I think it can be fixed. I have good friends, present company included, and a chance to get my license back. What more could a man want."

"Are you okay, Cam? This isn't like you."

"This is the new me. I won't let anything get me down."

"What-ever," Diane said skeptically.

"Come on and eat and then we'll go see Dave. If Jenny is the girl who was with Jack, then we are one step closer to solving this mystery. If she isn't, then I'm gonna' get laid tonight. Win-win."

"Cam, please," Diane said, putting her hands over her ears. "Too much info."

We attacked our breakfast voraciously, not talking until we'd finished. We lay down our forks at the same time and looked at each other.

"Was that good for you?" I said, knowing it would make her blush.

"Oh please," she said, covering her ears again. "What's gotten into you?"

I laughed. "Okay, I'm sorry. I'm just feeling a little slaphappy today I guess."

"Yeah, I guess."

We cleared the table together and washed the dishes and pans. I wiped down the table and centered the flowers. When I looked up, Diane was staring at me.

"I like the new Cam," she said. "That is if he didn't talk."

I put my finger and thumb together and drew them across my mouth like a zipper.

"That's better," she said.

We showered and had another cup of coffee.

"Do you have the picture of Jenny?" I asked Diane.

"Right here," she said, holding it up to reassure me of her competence.

I looked at it. Jenny was so beautiful, and I had really become quite attached to her. I hoped she was not tied to the boat jacking ring.

"Okay then, let's go."

We took my Mercedes and put the top down. Morning on Key West was the best time for a convertible. We rode in silence through the dock areas and into old town. The traffic was heavy, but we easily found a parking spot close to the marina.

We walked down the weathered board dock past numerous bars and cafés toward Schooners. I was dreading showing Dave the picture. Every step I took my legs got weaker. I was starting to get a little queasy in my stomach. I realized that I must care for Jenny even more than I thought.

We stepped in Schooners and approached the bar. Sammy and Pirate were sitting at the cigar booth, reading the paper.

"Hey, Sammy," I said, regressing again.

He looked up, and at the same time, Pirate looked up as if I had intruded in his space while he was reading the paper.

"Hey, Pirate," I said.

"Awwk, hey," Pirate said.

"Hiya, Cam," Sammy said and gave Pirate some kind of a treat. "Hiya, Diane," he said, tipping his pirate hat.

"Is Dave around? I have something I want to show him," I said.

"Nope, I'm afraid not," and he chuckled. "Dave's in the hospital."

"What's wrong with him? Is he okay?"

"His wife attacked him in his sleep. Hit him right on the head with a frying pan."

I remembered what Danny had told me about Dave and crazy Wanda going fishing and Dave's wife being ready to kill him.

"Is he conscious?"

"Don't know. I haven't talked to him," and Sammy laughed again. "Crazy bitch."

"Awwk, crazy bitch."

We left the comedy team and drove to the hospital.

The elderly lady at the reception desk directed us to the elevator and told us Dave was in room 214. We thanked her and took the steps. It's an old habit we have of walking up one flight and down two. It's supposed to keep you in shape, and it would if you did it more than once a month.

When we got to room 214, the door was closed. The attending nurse sat at a desk across from his room.

"May I help you?" she asked.

"Yes, I hope so. We are here to see Dave Richards," I said.

"I'm sorry but Dave cannot see anyone yet. Doctor's orders. He took quite a blow to the head."

I didn't really see how that would make any difference with the Dave Richards I knew.

"I'll only be a minute. It's very important. Just one question."

"Sorry, but Dave wouldn't be able to answer any questions. And if he did, you couldn't really count on it being the right answer."

"When do you think we will be able to see him?"

"My guess would be and remember it's only a guess, about two weeks. I've seen head injuries like his take longer," she said.

I thanked her, and we left the hospital feeling a little depressed.

"I thought we'd have an answer today," I said somberly.

"I thought you weren't going to let anything get you down," Diane said.

"You're absolutely right," and I straightened up and smiled. "Just because I don't really know the answer doesn't mean I can't get laid."

"Oh, Jesus," she said and shook her head.

Chapter 59

It was a quarter 'til eleven, and I was supposed to meet Sheriff Buck at eleven at my boat. I dropped Diane off at her house and drove to my dock.

The camera crews had diminished significantly. Only two reporters remained, and both stuck their microphones in my face as soon as I got out of my car.

"Did you know Tom Burnikel?" one of them asked.

"Who's Tom Burnikel?" I answered.

"The man killed in your boat," he said.

"No, I didn't know him."

The other man said, "What do you think of the allegations that you might have planted the bomb yourself to collect on the insurance?"

"What? Who said that?" I snapped angrily.

"It came from the sheriff's deputy, Billie Daryl Dunn."

"Not true and no further comments," I said, speeding my pace and looking for Sheriff Buck.

He was standing on the patio of my boat, talking to someone inside. When I approached, he turned and grinned. "Good morning, Cam," he said.

"What the hell is this about me planting the bomb to collect on the insurance?" I said, getting in his face.

"Whoa there, son, what are you talking about?"

"The reporters wanted to know what I thought about the sheriff's department claiming that I planted the bomb."

"I never told them anything of the kind."

"It was Billie Daryl," I said.

"Sorry about that, Cam. The boy's an idiot. I'll have a talk with him, and the reporters," he said, looking at the lot where they were standing.

"Now," I yelled. "Tell them now before they print it."

"Okay, calm down," and he stepped off the boat and ambled toward the reporters.

"What else can go wrong?" I asked myself. So much for not letting life get me down. There were just too many forces working against me.

Sheriff Buck returned and said, "That should hold them for a while. I told them anything they'd heard so far was inconclusive, and if they printed it, they would be obstructing justice."

"INCONCLUSIVE, WHAT DO YOU MEAN INCONCLUSIVE?"

"Okay, Cam. You're going to have to quit using that tone with me. I told you I stopped them."

"People are going to think I have something to hide. This could ruin my career."

"Don't let it get to you, Cam. We'll get it straightened out."

I couldn't believe it. It was like the sheriff wanted people to think I might have had something to do with this.

"Now, what we do know is that the man's name was Tom Burnikel. Pretty much a petty thief. He was probably trying to find something of value in there when the bomb went off."

"But he had to have brought the bomb on the boat with him," I said, trying to reason with him.

"Why would he do that?"

"I don't know. Maybe someone hired him to blow it up."

"Well, the bomb was in the nightstand next to the bed. If he was going to blow it up, wouldn't he just place the bomb in the middle of the living area and leave?"

"I don't know. I've never blown up a boat before," I said.

"Before what?"

I just looked at him in disbelief. I knew it was time to shut up.

"Are you charging me with anything?"

"Of course not, Cam," he said as if I had insulted him.

"Then why do you act as if I had something to do with this?"

"I'm just trying to eliminate you as a suspect. That's all."

Chapter 60

Sanchez pulled the report from the fax machine and returned to his office. Agent Wootton was sitting across from him, drinking his coffee and eating a donut.

Sanchez looked at him in disgust. "If you don't stop eating those things you're going to explode."

Agent Wootton, it seemed, never ate right. He couldn't pass up a hot dog stand and always had a half-eaten donut on his desk. Still, he had the body of a twenty-year-old athlete; muscular arms, defined chest, square jaw. It wasn't fair.

"And you'll die of stress if you don't quit worrying about everyone else," he said while stuffing the rest of the donut in his mouth.

Sanchez read the report and handed it to Wootton.

When Wootton finished reading it, he laid it down on the desk.

"That is one screwed up son of a bitch," Wootton said.

"Yeah, not only did he kill Amar's daughter but he convinced him that Ted did it. Then he threw in the rest of the squad so Amar would want to kill them all. Buck has been working on this for a long time. How do you suppose he got flipped to the Al-Qaeda?"

"I don't know. The report didn't mention him spending any time with them."

"The Commander of his squad said Buck was a loose cannon. He was always starting fights with the rest of the men, and when they got ambushed while on a mission, Ted blamed Buck for talking to Amar's family about where they'd be."

"Do you think he did?"

"I do now. That's when Buck killed her and made it look like Ted had done it."

"Maybe we can convince Amar that Buck was the one who killed his daughter and he would call off the attack on Quantico," Wootton said.

261

"No, I don't think he would believe us. Anyway, we need to know where that bomb is and when he's going to pick it up. Otherwise, we would have arrested him long ago. Whoever is building this bomb can do it again and has probably done it before."

"So, Buck killed Amar's daughter so Amar would revenge her death. Amar was wealthy enough to get their plan rolling, but they still needed more money, and that's when they started stealing boats," Wootton theorized aloud.

"Looks that way. Susan Crane told us that she and Bill had a good little business going along with the help of John Trapper. Then John brought Buck in, and they started stealing boats and killing the owners," Sanchez said. "She said they didn't know about killing anyone until two weeks ago. That's when they decided to get out."

"Maybe they didn't."

Sanchez's cell phone rang. He picked it up and looked at the caller ID. "It's Utley," he said.

"Sanchez," he answered.

"I'm watching Amar. He cruised up the coast last night, blacked out. I think this might be it," Utley said. "Right now he's anchored one mile off the coast of Miami."

"Don't get too close, but don't lose him. I haven't heard from Agent Anderson. Is Buck with Amar?"

"No, just him and Kasim."

"Okay, let me know if he turns into port anywhere, and I'll make sure they're watched once on land."

"Will do," Utley said and hung up.

"It won't be long now," Sanchez said.

Chapter 61

Later that day, Diane and I were sitting at Sloppy Joe's, having a drink and listening to a guitar player named Troy from Evansville, Indiana.

He was pretty damn good. It made you wonder how good you had to be to make it in Nashville. Most of the talent I'd heard around here sounded as good as anyone I'd heard on the radio. Watching him made me think of my good Taylor guitar laying in pieces scattered around my boat.

"Hi, Cam, Diane," I heard Jenny say.

I turned to see her standing beside me. I rose and pulled out a chair for her, bowed and motioned for her to sit. She did.

"Well, aren't you the gentleman," she said, feigning that southern drawl she sometimes used.

"I wondered when I was going to see you," I said.

Jenny said, ignoring my flirtation, "Do you have your hands full comforting Cam?"

"Of course. It's like the whole world blew up instead of one rusty old boat," Diane said.

"Men," Jenny emphasized.

"Yeah, men."

"Wait a minute, girls. I'm not without my good points you know."

"Name one," Jenny said.

"I can make you laugh when we're making love."

"Oh yes, there is that," Jenny said.

"Okay, I have things to do and places to go," Diane said, getting up and pouring the rest of her drink down her throat.

"Oh don't go," I said, "I'll be good."

"No, really, I've got to go," she said and hugged me and then Jenny.

"Alright, maybe I'll see you tonight," I said.

"Bye, Diane," Jenny yelled as she hurried out the door.

"She doesn't like to hear about my love life," I said to Jenny.

"Maybe she has a crush on you."

"No, she thinks of me as her father."

"I wouldn't be too sure about that."

Changing the subject, I said, "So, what have you been up to?"

"Nothing much. I didn't buy that Tiger boat I was looking at. They wanted too much for it."

"You'll know when the right one comes along. What do you know about the man who had the boat for sale?" I said, prying a little and hoping to get some insight.

I still needed to know that Jenny was not entangled in the boat thefts. I needed one thing in my life to be real, and the FBI had indicated to Chad that there was a lot more to it than the theft of some luxury yachts.

"Nothing really. He's an executive for an aircraft restoring company. It's a company boat, and they want to sell it," she replied.

"Have you tried making him a lower offer?"

"I tried, but we were too far apart."

"Too bad," I said, wanting to pry further but afraid of losing her if she did have something to hide, and afraid of getting too close to her also if she was hiding something I might not want to know.

"Would you like to have dinner with me tonight? I'll take you to the best restaurant in town. I still have a little of my expense account left from

New York," I said, deciding I'd pried enough for now.

"I'm sorry, Cam, but I am going to be leaving for a week. I have to go back to Michigan to tie up some loose ends on my transfer of the hedge funds. I leave this evening."

"Oh, I didn't know. How about a drink right now then and a rain check for when you get back?"

"You're on," she said, but her eyes were saying goodbye.

Chapter 62

After our drink, I kissed Jenny goodbye and wandered down to the dock area, four blocks away.

I saw Sammy and Pirate coming toward me, talking to each other. There were some really quirky people in Key West.

"Hey ya, Cam," Sammy said.

"Hey ya, Cam, awk," Pirate copied.

"How are you guys doing?" I asked.

If Pirate would have started talking first, telling me how they'd had a bad day, I wouldn't have been surprised.

"Not bad, and guess what?"

"What?"

"Dave woke up," he said, tapping me on the chest with his long finger as if to drive the point home.

"You don't say. You think I can go see him?" I asked.

"Yep. Crazy Wanda did. She said he was normal. Not even a bump on his head."

"What about his wife? Did she know Crazy Wanda went to see him?"

"Yep, said she don't care."

"Thank you, Sammy. Now, if you'll excuse me, I need to go."

"Tell him 'ol Sammy and Pirate say 'Hey'," Sammy said.

"Hey, awk."

"Will do."

~*~

Jenny arrived at Buck's house at four-thirty.
She wasn't looking forward to this. She knew the time was close and it could get very dangerous. What if Juba wanted to tie up all the loose ends? She was alone here with no protection.

269

Buck opened the door and smiled at her. "Hello, Jenny, come on in and have a celebratory drink," he said, opening the door wider and stepping aside.

"What are we celebrating?" she asked, entering the house.

"The end of an era. No more boat thefts, no more killing innocent people, and the countdown to the end of our mission."

"So, the bomb is ready?"

"Yes, it is. And in two days it will be on the way to Quantico."

"What will my part be in these last few days?"

"Your part," Buck said, handing her a drink. "Your part is over, my child."

"But there has to be something I can do. I can help you deliver the bomb, or maybe watch your back. I can shoot a rifle with the best of them."

"I'm afraid I have Billie Daryl for that. If we have too many people then things get too complicated," he said, holding his hands out to the side as if it were out of his control.

Jenny took a big drink of her Wild Turkey and sat the glass down on the table. "Well, I guess this is goodbye then," she said.

"Wait just a minute, I have something for you."

He turned, opened a cabinet and reached inside. Jenny, at the same time, reached in her purse and gripped the handle of her Glock 19.

Buck turned, a package in his hand. His eyes went straight to Jenny's purse. He smiled. "Darling, do you really think I would harm you? I've grown quite fond of you. And if I we're going to kill you, it wouldn't be in my own house."

"You never know in this business," Jenny said. "What's in the package?"

Buck handed it to her and said, "Severance. I hope one hundred thousand will tide you over until you get a new job."

"Well, it certainly won't hurt," Jenny said, dropping the package into her purse.

"I'm going to miss you," he said. "We could have done a lot of business together if we would have met earlier."

"It's not too late."

"Yes, it is too late. My business days are almost over."

Jenny didn't like the sound of that. Was he going to deliver the bomb personally and blow himself up with the rest of the base?

Chapter 63

I left the hospital with Jenny's picture in my pocket. I felt sick to my stomach. Dave had confirmed that Jenny was the girl he saw walk Jack to the boat. What was Jenny doing with Jack on that dock, and what happened to Jack? Was she the last one to see him alive? Did she kill him?

I pondered these questions and at the same time tried to figure out what to do with the information. Did Jenny have anything to do with my boat blowing up? All these questions kept coming to my mind as I drove north on Highway 1. I turned into the sheriff's station without even thinking about what I was doing. I guess I knew what I had to do with the new facts.

Deputy Wilson was working at the front desk when I entered. I had seen him around town quite often and had played cards with him on a few occasions.

"Hi, Brent, how are you?" I said politely as I approached the desk.

"Pretty good, Cam. What brings you to this part of town?"

"I need to see Sheriff Buck. Is he in?"

"No, but he'll be back in an hour or so. Can I help you with something?"

"Do you have an envelope and a pen and paper? I'll just leave him a message."

"Sure," Brent said and handed me the paper and pen. "I'll be right back with the envelope."

I wrote a note to Buck explaining the picture of Jenny and what Dave had told me about her and Jack. That was all I could say because I didn't really have any further facts. Just speculation.

Brent returned with the envelope and handed it to me.

I folded the note, inserted it into the envelope and then started to slip the picture in. Jenny's face stared up at me. I felt sick again.

"Are you okay, Cam?" Brent asked.

I looked at him for a minute, not registering what he'd said, but then came back from wherever I had been. "Yeah, I'm good," I said, sliding the picture in and sealing the envelope.

I handed it to Brent and asked him to give it to Buck.

"I will. As soon as he walks in."

"Thanks."

"Hey, Dan's having a card game next week. You going?"

"Maybe. I don't know yet," I said somberly.

"If you do, bring plenty of quarters. I'm feeling lucky," and he chuckled.

"I'll only need the one, then I can play with yours."

I waved bye to him and walked back out into the humid evening air. It was hard to breathe. "Must be the humidity," I told myself.

I drove back to Diane's house, poured a stiff Wild Turkey and took it out to the back patio. Diane wasn't home, so I took the opportunity to mellow. I must have needed the drink and quiet. The next thing I knew Diane was waking me and telling me it was time for bed.

Chapter 64

Agent Wootton walked into Sanchez's office and slapped a paper down on his desk. "Check it out," he said. "This just came in. Buck was a college roommate with Yazid Bishara. We checked, and he is known to be connected to the Taliban."

"The Taliban," Sanchez said.

"Yeah. We figure that is when Buck was recruited. Yazid must have convinced him that the US was killing innocent Muslims or something to that effect. William Buck and Yazid Bishara started an organized march at WVU, to recruit followers and sympathy for Jihad."

"Holy war?" Sanchez said.

"Right. And guess who was arrested in 2005 for smuggling C4 to a militant group called the Islamic Jihad Union?"

"Buck," Sanchez guessed.

"No, Michael Garrison, only you know him as Billie Daryl Dunn. He changed his name, not legally, after doing twenty-four months in prison, and then disappeared. In 2008 he joined the sheriff's department in Key West, a year after William Buck became Chief. He works at the docks most of the time, but Buck swears him in when he needs him."

"Oh shit. This is getting complicated. We have an invisible terrorist organization working right here in Key West."

"Yeah, right, but we knew that already. We just didn't know who was involved."

"The IJU has terrorist cells in Kyrgyzstan, Uzbekistan, and Russia. They have bombed the US and Israeli embassies among other attacks and were seen fighting alongside the Taliban."

"Cam Derringer is right in the middle of all this. If he goes to Buck and tells him he knows that his girlfriend Jenny is involved in the boat jacking, Buck will kill him."

"We need to get him out of there before it's too late," Sanchez said.

"I'll have one of my men pick him up."

"On what charges?"

"We'll think of something."

"What about Buck?" Sanchez said, thinking out loud.

"We can't tip our hand yet. We don't want to alert Amar before we find that bomb."

"Yeah I know but..."

"We'll protect Cam and Jenny," Wootton said.

Chapter 65

The next morning, I woke late. The sun was shining in my window, and it felt warm and comforting.

It was a muggy day, as most were, and I still found it hard to breathe. My guess was I wouldn't be able to breathe right again until I'd found out what had happened to Jack.

I walked through the house, looking for Diane.

"DIANE?" I repeated twice.

No answer so I walked through the living room and into the kitchen. I heard music coming from the back yard, so I opened the back door and stepped out.

Diane was lying on a chaise lounge, scarcely clad in a bikini.

"HELLO," I said loud enough for her to hear but not so loud as to scare her.

She didn't hear me. I walked around her to the front of her chair. She was asleep, and with the music, couldn't hear anything.

I had a little dilemma. I didn't want to scare her by touching her and didn't want to yell louder. That would scare her too. I didn't want her to wake up and see me standing here staring at her either. Kind of a catch-22.

I stood there for a second and couldn't help but look at her magnificent body. It looked as if it were sculpted by an artist. She was very fit, and her six-pack was quite defined. Her long legs were…

"What are you looking at?" I heard her say.

I jumped. Now I was the one who ended up getting scared.

"I...I didn't want to scare you," I said, in what I thought sounded like a very guilty voice.

"Uh-huh," she said with a crooked smile.

"I wanted to fill you in on the latest," I said, trying to change the subject.

"And you were going to do that by staring at me while I slept," she said, still smiling.

"No. I didn't know what to do. I didn't want to scare you," I said, still stumbling through my words.

"Just kidding, but you do sound guilty."

"Okay, you got me," I said, raising my hands in surrender.

"Pervert."

"Anyway, I wanted to fill you in on the latest."

"Alright," she said, not making any attempt to cover up.

"After you left Sloppy Joe's yesterday, Jenny told me she was going to leave last night for Michigan for a week. I went to the docks to see if anything new had come up when I ran into Sammy and Pirate. He said Dave had woken up, so I took the picture of Jenny to the hospital and Dave ID'ed her as the woman Jack had left with."

"Oh no, Cam. I'm sorry. I know that must hurt."

"Yeah, it does, but what really hurts is that I turned her in to Buck."

"You did the right thing, Cam."

"Maybe, I hope I didn't react too quickly."

"When was Jenny supposed to leave?"

"Last night."

"But I saw her last night. I drove past her house on my way home, and she was going in the front door."

"Are you sure?"

"Yes, it was around ten."

I was just about to ask why she was going past Jenny's house when I heard a car door close in the driveway.

"I'll go see who it is," I said, "You cover up."

"I was dressed fine a minute ago."

"Cover up," I said, throwing her a towel that was hanging over another chair.

I went through the kitchen and peeked into the driveway from the side window. I recognized the black SUV and the suited men as FBI. They would stand out in church. I didn't like this. Since I'd returned to Key West, no one had asked me about finding Barbie.

They apparently knew I'd returned to work on the boat case. That's why they'd had me in New York in the first place, to stop me.

I returned to Diane in the back yard, closing the door quietly.

"It's the FBI," I said in her ear. "I've got to get out of here."

"I'll hold them off," Diane whispered back. "Go over the fence and down the alley. Call me later, and I'll come get you."

"Forget everything I told you about Jenny. We can't pass that on to them."

"No problem. Now go," she said, standing and going to the back door.

"Cover up," I said.

She smiled and put her hand on her hips in a pose. "I said I was going to hold them off."

I turned and ran toward the back gate. When I came to it, I hurdled it instead of opening it.

Chapter 66

I ran for three blocks before stopping to catch my breath. I was in the middle of a tourist group who were taking pictures of a street performer, painted silver and posing like a statue. Some of the things people thought of. I stood in the crowd and looked up and down the street, half expecting the FBI to come racing in their SUV's, blasting bullets from machine guns out the open doors.

I waited five minutes before walking down the street toward the southernmost point. It was the most out of the way place I could think of in this area. No one would just happen by there. It was a destination.

I entered a bar close to the street where I could sit at a table with a view. The windows, which had no glass, only shutters, were open. I ordered a Diet Coke and some chips—the breakfast of champions.

Looking out the window, I watched groups of tourist taking turns standing at the southernmost point monument and paying a lady, who spent her days standing there waiting for this opportunity, to take their pictures with their own cameras.

Halfway through my breakfast, my cell phone rang. I didn't recognize the number on my caller I.D. but answered it anyway. Even if it was the FBI, I could just hang up.

"Hello."

"Cam, it's Buck."

"Willie, I'm glad to hear from you. Did you get my message?"

"Yes, I did. Are you sure?"

"I only know what I told you. Except Diane said she saw Jenny late last night entering her house and Jenny had told me she was leaving for Michigan yesterday."

"Do you have any other proof that Jenny could be involved in this?" Buck asked.

"Well, I saw her meeting with those Iraqi men, but you said you'd checked them out and they seemed legitimate."

"Yeah, they did. I hope you're not just jumping to conclusions. I don't want to insinuate anything, but maybe Jenny has another guy, and she just needed some space for a while."

I gave that some thought. "Maybe, but what about Jack and her on the docks? She was the last person to be seen with him."

"Sounds like you're sure she's involved," Buck said.

"I'm afraid so."

"Where are you?"

"I'm hiding from the FBI right now. They're at Diane's house looking for me."

"Why does the FBI want you?"

"It's a long story. To make it short, they think I'm getting too close to the truth about the boat jacking ring, and they want me out of their way."

There was a brief silence on the other end of the line.

"Where did you say you were?" Buck asked.

"I didn't say."

"Cam, I can offer you some protection. I'll make sure they don't find you."

"I can't take the chance right now, Willie. I know you're only looking out for me, but I need to be able to move around on my own for a while."

"I want you to come to my house tonight. Don't tell a soul you're coming. I won't try to talk you into turning yourself in, but we need to talk. It sounds like you're in trouble and I want to help you. Maybe together we can find out who is behind this."

"We'll see. Give me some time to think about it."

When they hung up, Buck called Jenny.

Chapter 67

Jenny picked up the phone on the first ring.
"Hello."

"Hello, sweetheart," Buck said.

"Juba, what a pleasure. Did you miss me already?"

"I missed you before you left."

"So, did you decide you needed me?" Jenny said.

"That I did. We have a bit of a problem. Do you still want to help?"

"Of course I do."

"Good. This is for your good too."

"Sounds important."

"Very. I just talked to Cam. He has a picture of you and Jack on the dock together on the day he disappeared."

"How did he get that?" Jenny asked, surprised.

"I'm not sure, but I have the picture or at least a copy."

"That is a problem?"

"Yeah, and it gets worse."

"Tell me."

"He said the FBI is after him. They think he's getting too close to the boat jacking case."

"The FBI?"

"Right. We need to get him before they do."

"Get him?"

"Diane saw you going into your house last night after you left here."

"That's not good. I wonder what she was doing at my house?"

"I don't know."

"I bet she was waiting to see if I was with Cam. I think she's developed a thing for him."

"I know you and Cam got close, but this could jeopardize the whole operation. If we get him and hold him somewhere until it is all over, we'll be able to let him go. I don't want to harm him."

"How are we going to do that?"

"That's where you come in."

~*~

I finished my breakfast of chips and diet coke. I had been here for an hour and was reasonably sure the FBI had left Diane's house by now. I'd pulled out my cell phone to call her when it rang. According to the caller ID, it was Jenny. I had to be careful how I talked to her now. I didn't want her to know that I suspected her.

"Jenny. How was your flight?"

"Hi, Cam. I didn't go."

Now I was confused again. She's not lying to me. Was she ever? Still, there was the picture.

"Why not? Did something happen?"

"Yes, you happened."

"Me?"

"Yes. After I had left you yesterday, I did a lot of thinking. I want to stay here and give us a try. That is if you want me to."

My mind was reeling. I did want us to give it a try, but I still wasn't sure about her. This would, however, give me a chance to find out one way or the other.

"Sure," I heard myself say hesitantly.

"Are you sure?"

"Yes," I said more assuredly.

"Great. Where are you? I'll come and get you, and we'll go have brunch somewhere."

"Why don't I just meet you at the Harpoon Café in twenty minutes?"

"Alright. I'll see you then."

"Goodbye," I said, but she had already hung up.

Chapter 68

The Harpoon Café was only a block away. I paid my tab and carefully stepped out of my hiding place and onto the sidewalk.

Looking both ways, like a good scout, I crossed the street and made my way down the block. I knew I would be like a needle in a haystack for the FBI to find. I felt reasonably safe for now.

I called Diane to fill her in on the latest development. Her cell phone rang six times and then went to voice mail. I hung up. That was unusual for her. She knew I was going to call her.

The Harpoon Café was in the next block. I slowed my steps and slid inside a doorway. I thought it was best not to enter until Jenny did. I had a good view of the front door from here but was hidden from view to anyone entering the café.

Fifteen minutes went by when a black SUV stopped three doors down from the café, and two suited men got out.

They crossed the street to the café and entered. A minute later, they came back out and looked up and down the street. I slid back in the doorway further.

They were most definitely the FBI. How did they find me so fast?

I then remembered how they had tapped my phone in New York. I took my phone from my pocket and dropped it in a trashcan next to the door. I could always get a burn phone.

Jenny sat in her car and watched the FBI enter the café and return. Cam wasn't with them. She surveyed the street. It was busy with tourists, but she saw him standing in a doorway a block away.

I left the safety of the doorway and hurriedly walked back in the direction I had come from.

I had gone a block when a horn honked, and I saw Jenny waving at me.

"Hey, Cam, hop in," she said.

I did.

"I saw you walking so I thought I'd pick you up."

"Thanks," I said, and kissed her on the cheek.

"Why were you walking away from the restaurant? Did you change your mind?"

"No, of course not. I forgot my cell phone and was going to run back down to the bar to get it."

"The bar? So early?" she teased.

She stopped in front of it, and I went in supposedly to retrieve my cell phone. I stood inside a moment, watching her through the window.

I returned to her car and told her my phone was gone.

"Well that sucks," she said.

"Yeah. You can't leave anything lying around these days."

"Do you still feel like breakfast?"

"Sure, I'm hungry. What about you?"

"Fine by me. How about my house? I have bacon and eggs in the fridge."

"Let's go," I said, welcoming normalcy back into my life for a few minutes.

Chapter 69

I watched Jenny working in the kitchen. She looked lovely in the way she orchestrated the simple task of preparing breakfast. I was now officially hooked on her. She turned and smiled at me.

"What are you looking at?" she said.

That instantly reminded me of Diane. I needed to try to get in touch with her again.

I smiled but didn't say anything. She turned back to her cooking.

"May I borrow your phone," I asked. "I need to call Diane."

"Sure," she said, retrieving her phone from her purse.

"Thank you. I'll only be a minute."

I walked to the back porch and dialed Diane's number. Still no answer after four rings. I then heard an incoming call and automatically looked at the caller ID. W. Buck was printed across the screen.

What was that about, I wondered? I ignored the call and let the phone ring for Diane four more times. Still no answer.

I returned to the kitchen and laid the phone down on the table.

"Any luck?" Jenny asked.

"No, she still doesn't answer, but you missed a call while I was trying," I said. "Sorry I don't know who it was," I lied.

She picked up her phone and checked her missed calls.

"My partner in Michigan," she said. "They're not too crazy about the fact I didn't show up for the meeting."

"I hope you're not going to have trouble because you stayed here with me. You know you can go back for a week and then we can pick up where we left off."

"I just don't want to leave you."

"It's only a week."

"Yeah, you're probably right."

She placed the bacon and eggs on a plate and sat it on the table.

"Pour yourself some juice, and I'll return this call real quick. I'll be right back," and she walked to the back porch.

I busied myself eating breakfast and wondering what her business with Sheriff Buck could be. Whatever it was, she didn't want me to know.

If Buck was following up on my hunch, I don't think he would just call her, and why was his name entered in her phonebook?

"You must have been hungry," she said from behind me as she came back in the kitchen.

I looked down at my plate. It was empty. I hadn't even noticed I'd finished.

'I'm sorry. I should have waited for you. I didn't even know I was eating."

She laughed, "That's okay. Would you like some more?"

"No thanks. I think I had better get going. I need to find Diane."

"Oh, don't go yet," she said.

"I really need to," I said, getting up.

She put her arms around me and gave me a long, sensual kiss on the lips.

"Are you sure you need to go," she said in a sultry voice.

I thought about it for a moment and then pulled her arms away. "Yes, I'm afraid I have to, but please remember where we left off for when I return."

"I will," she said. "Do you want a ride?"

"No, I think I'll walk back to her house and get my car."

"Okay, be careful," she said in what sounded like a worried voice.

~*~

I'd walked out the front door and down the street a block and a half when Sheriff Buck pulled up beside me in his car.

I waved, and he motioned for me to get in. I didn't have much choice so opened the door and took a seat next to the large man.

"What's up?" I asked.

"Cam, I'm sorry, but I have a warrant for your arrest."

"On what charges?"

"It seems the insurance investigators think you blew up your boat to collect the insurance. That means Tom Burnikel's death was murder, even if you didn't know he was there."

"That's crazy. I didn't blow up my own boat."

"Maybe not, but right now you have to come with me."

I was in shock. How could this happen?

"Do I need to cuff you or will you come peacefully?"

"I'll go with you. I'll be out in a few hours," I said, already planning my defense.

"I'm not going to take you to the jailhouse. I'm taking you to my own house. I don't want to ruin your reputation until we're sure. I owe you that much. We've been friends for a long time."

That really seemed strange to me. How was he going to explain to the court that he'd executed the warrant?

We pulled into his garage, and the door closed behind us.

"Let's go," he said, getting out.

I followed him into the house. Jenny was sitting on the sofa.

Chapter 70

Lieutenant Utley had his binoculars trained on the fifty-two foot, Tiger.

"It's been sitting there for a full day now," Utley said to Agent McComas of the FBI, "and we haven't seen any sign of life."

"They're still there. They're just laying low until the time comes. Let me see your binoculars," he said, pulling them from Utley's grasp.

McComas put the binoculars to his eyes and watched the Tiger.

"They're probably below deck watching...**Oh!**" he yelled. "**It just blew up.**"

A second later, they heard the explosion and shortly after felt the concussion.

"What the hell," Utley said. "Give me those binoculars."

McComas handed them back without taking his eyes off the boat, now a ball of fire.

"Shit," Utley said.

He turned to the first mate, "Get that anchor up and tell Hollencamp to head for the boat."

He then grabbed his mic and announced, "Man fire stations. Be ready to pump jets."

"Not much need for that, Lieutenant," McComas said. "The boat is gone."

Utley turned back to look. He held his binoculars an inch below his eyes and peered over the top at the spot where the fifty-two foot Tiger had been. It was gone, only a small flame coming from what was left of it.

Utley picked up his cell phone and called Sanchez.

"**What do you** mean gone?" Sanchez asked excitedly.

"It blew up and sank. We're on the way, but I don't think we're going to find anyone," Utley said, waiting for the yelling to begin.

"You didn't see any other boats approach it did you?"

"Not a thing. We've been watching it constantly."

"Shit. If they got off, we don't have any idea where they are."

"We're approaching now. I'll call you back," Utley said and hung up.

~*~

Six hours earlier:

Amar stepped onto the first rung of the ladder leading to the wooden dock. He climbed up and turned so Kasim could hand him a bag. Amar laid it on the dock and helped Kasim up the ladder.

Together, they removed their wetsuits and tanks. They tied them together and dropped them into a weighted bag that had been waiting for them on the dock. Kasim dropped the bag into the water and watched it sink.

Picking up their bag, Kasim held it open for Amar.

He reached in and removed their wallets and a hard case containing seven hundred thousand dollars.

"Let's go," Amar said.

The white van was waiting for them right where they were told it would be. Amar checked the wheel well and found the keys.

"It's a beautiful night," Amar said, looking up to the heavens.

Chapter 71

Sanchez called agent Wootton into his office. If they were going to have any chance of stopping the bombing now, they had to find Amar.

Sanchez filled Wootton in on what had happened.

"I want you to go to the dock area nearest to where the boat blew up and see if you can turn up any surveillance cameras," Sanchez said. "Check all the businesses in the area. If they got off the boat, it was between ten o'clock last night and eleven today."

"Alright, I'll put some men on it. Do we have any idea what area the bomb might be in?"

"No, I'm waiting for Agent Anderson to check in. We might know something by this evening.

Meantime, I'm going down to the dock area myself. I'll check all penetration points and see if I can find a clue as to where they might have come ashore."

"Have you warned Quantico yet?" Wootton asked.

"No. I didn't want to cause an alarm, but I think I might have to now."

"Contact Commander Bosse. He's a straight shooter and is in command of the base. I believe we should also contact Ted Trueblood. He knows Buck as well as anyone. He might be able to give us a little insight."

Sanchez called Quantico and asked for Commander Bosse.

"Yes," Bosse said in a gruff voice.

"Commander, this is Special Agent in Charge Carlos Sanchez, of the FBI."

"What can I do for you, Mister Sanchez?"

"Do you remember William Buck?"

There was a pause on Bosse's end.

"Why do you want to know?" Bosse eventually said.

"I have reason to believe that he and Amar Mustafa are planning to blow you and Trueblood and the rest of the base to smithereens."

"You have my full attention. I know him."

"We were following Amar but lost him. He is somewhere in Miami. We think he is there to purchase a bomb big enough for the job."

"He's acquiring a bomb, and you lost him," Bosse said sharply.

"He's good, but that's beside the point. The point is, we need to protect your base."

"He's not going to get on this base. We have top-notch security," Bosse said.

"Did you or did you not send William Buck an invitation to a squadron reunion?"

"Well, yeah. We sent one to everybody from our platoon."

"There you go. Buck doesn't have to sneak onto the base. He was invited."

"What makes you think they want to blow up the base?"

"They've been planning an attack for eight years. They were planning it while they were in Iraq."

"Why didn't you stop them earlier?"

"We didn't know what the target was until last week. They probably didn't even know what they were going to hit until recently.

"Why are they getting the bomb all the way down in Miami if they are planning to use it here? Couldn't they get one closer to Quantico?"

"We've been asking ourselves that very same question. All I can tell you is our information comes from a member of their group," Sanchez said.

"Can you count on that info?"

"No, not entirely, but that's all we have."

"What if they are planning to blow something up between Miami and Quantico and they just want you to think it's here?"

"That's a possibility, but we can't protect the whole east coast."

"Does it concern you at all that the President and his family are arriving at Miami Beach in two days' time for vacation, and that the president himself will be playing golf at the Miami Beach Golf Club?"

"We've got it covered."

"And the Presidential Yacht?"

"Safe also," Sanchez said.

"You know he would be a more likely target than us."

"Of course we know that. We have very tight security appointed for him."

"Tight enough for a very large bomb?" Bosse asked.

Chapter 72

"Hello Jenny," I said. "Imagine seeing you here."

"It's not what you think, Cam."

"I saw your caller ID earlier. I know Buck called you and you called him back. Why did you turn me in? I would have come in on my own accord if I would have known there was a warrant for my arrest."

"There is no warrant for you, Cam," Buck said.

"Then why am I here?"

"You've gotten too close to the truth. It was only a matter of time before you would have been telling the FBI that Jenny was involved in the boat jacking."

"Then it's true. You are involved in it," I said to Jenny.

"You could say that," she said.

"And all of this between us, what was that all about? Just wanting to keep an eye on me?"

"It started that way, but I really do have feelings for you now."

"Screw you," I said to her, pointing my middle finger to the sky for emphasis.

I could see a tear forming in her eye. She looked away and dabbed at it with a tissue.

"What did you do with Jack?" I demanded.

Buck said, "That was most unfortunate. Jack had some critical key evidence against us that he wasn't willing to share."

"And you," I said, pointing to Buck, "You were in this from the beginning, along with Bill and Susan Crane."

"Now you know. I knew you'd figure it out eventually. That's why I had to bring you here," Buck said.

"So now you're going to kill me to keep me quiet."

"No, that's not the plan. We're just going to keep you here for a couple of days and then you will be free to go."

"You can't do that, and I know it."

"Yes we can," Jenny said. "I'll be long gone, and Juba will be…"

"That's right, Cam, I'll be dead. I'll be known as a suicide bomber."

I couldn't believe what I was hearing. It was too much to take in. Jenny was in a plot to blow up…what? And Buck was going to kill himself to do it.

"What are you going to blow up?" I asked but wasn't sure I wanted to know.

"Quantico," Jenny said.

Buck laughed. "All those miserable Marines who thought they had the right to kill my Farrah and then laugh about it. Amar, Farah's father, is going to help me. He is getting the bomb as we speak."

"You're not going to get away with this, Willie, or Juba or whatever name you want to be called. I'll make sure the world knows how you killed all those innocent people just to get their boats. They won't immortalize you. You'll go down as a terrorist."

"Yes, that is what I am," Buck said.

Then a terrible thought hit me, "What did you do with Diane?"

"We don't have her," Buck said. "I would never harm her."

~*~

Diane sat in the FBI office in Miami. She didn't know why she was here, but she knew Cam was in some danger.

Sanchez entered the room. "Hello, Diane, I'm Agent Sanchez."

"Why am I here and where is Cam?"

"We were going to ask you the same thing. Don't you know?"

"No, all I know is he was hiding from you. You'll never find him."

"Yes we will, and you better hope it is before Sheriff Buck does."

"Buck. What's he got to do with anything?"

"He is planning an attack on the United States. We think we know where but we're not sure. Right now, he thinks he is safe and that Cam is the only one who knows what he is planning to do. That's why we wanted to bring Cam in. It was for his own protection."

"How do you know all this?"

"We have an agent working close to Buck. Her name is Robin Anderson. You know her as Jenny Jacobs."

"Jenny is an FBI agent?"

"Yes she is, and I hope she can protect Cam. It won't be easy if Buck has him. Jenny might have to make a choice between Cam and a base full of a thousand Marines."

Chapter 73

Amar Mustafa and Kasim Maliki, Amar's brother-in-law, entered the warehouse on Miami's Little West River. Three men appeared from behind wooden crates, stacked to one side. They pointed their machine guns at the two men.

A fourth man walked into view from a darkened corner.

"Amar, it is good to see you. You are right on time."

"Good afternoon, Mister Simmons," Amar said.

"The bomb is ready; do you have the money?"

"Yes, we have the money."

"Good, I will take it now," Simmons said.

"It is close by. You will get it when I get the bomb," Amar said.

"You don't trust me," the man said and laughed.

"Why would I trust a man who builds a bomb and asks no questions as to what it will be used for, then raises the price after we had a deal."

"I could just kill you, you know," Simmons said.

"Then all you would have is a bomb and nothing to blow up."

The man went silent for a moment but then said, "Very well. Come with me."

He turned and walked back into the shadows and opened a door. They entered a dark room, and he closed the door behind them. He flipped a switch, and the room lit up.

At its center stood a large table. On it was a package, about three feet square. Wires were protruding from inside, running to a box taped to the exterior.

"That is your receiver," Simmons said, pointing to the exterior box. "Your cell phone is your sending unit," he said, handing Amar a phone number. "It works like the smaller bomb I gave you earlier. Just dial that number and hit send." He held his hands up and said, "Boom."

"Is it safe to transport?" Amar asked.

"How far are you planning to go with it?"

"All the way to Virginia," Amar said.

"Virginia?"

"Yes, is that a problem?"

"I could have made it for you in Virginia, but Juba said to make it here. It is very dangerous to travel that far with a bomb this size. That transmitter is not exclusive. This device can be triggered from any phone using that number."

"Then we had better hope we don't receive a wrong number," Amar said.

He turned to Kasim. "Go get the gentlemen their money. Would you and the other gentlemen please escort Kasim to get it?" he directed at Simmons. "I will lock the door behind us."

"You're one crazy son of a bitch," Simmons said to Amar.

Amar followed them out of the room. The other three joined them, and together they walked to the door leading out to the parking lot. Before they could open it, Amar pulled his forty-five caliber grease gun from under his robe and shot Simmons in the back. One of the men turned and started to raise his gun. Amar shot him in the head. A crimson spray covered the other two men, and they threw their arms up to protect their faces from the blood. Amar took the opportunity to shoot each of them in a short barrage of gunfire.

"I told you, Kasim, that I would kill them for raising the price," Amar said. "Now, let's roll the bomb to the van and get it loaded. We have to be at Miami Beach Mariana tomorrow to load it on the boat for Virginia."

Chapter 74

Commander Bosse called Sargent Ted Trueblood into his office. They were going to have to be ready for an attack even if the chances of it happening were slim.

Trueblood entered the room and saluted. Bosse returned it half-heartedly and told Ted to sit.

"We have a problem," Bosse said. "It's William Buck. He has a bomb—a *large* bomb. The FBI called and said they think his target is Quantico. He vowed revenge, and now I'm afraid he might try to get it."

"Why don't they just arrest him?"

"They don't have any proof yet that he is involved with the bomb. But guess who is supposedly picking it up as we speak?"

Trueblood stared at Bosse, blankly.

"Amar Mustafa," Bosse said.

"Amar? You mean they are still together?"

"Looks that way. I thought we had Amar convinced Buck was the one who killed his daughter, but I guess Buck convinced him otherwise."

"It's on record that Buck was the main suspect in the killing."

"The records don't mean a thing to a terrorist like Amar."

"He wasn't a terrorist until we killed his daughter," Trueblood said.

Bosse slammed his fist down on the desk. "I told you to never say we did that. Not even in private."

"Sorry, Sir."

Bosse sat back in his chair and tented his hands under his chin. "I have a mission for you," he said. "I want you to go find Buck before the FBI does. He needs to be silenced. It's for the good of the country. If he blows up Quantico and tells the world why, thousands of Marines could be killed, and we would be exposed. That would make us responsible for the attack."

"Silenced?" Trueblood said.

"Get your rifle. You're a sniper and a damn good one. Consider it a mission of national defense."

"Yes, Sir," Trueblood said, snapping to attention and saluting.

"I'll have a plane ready for you in one hour. He is in Key West. There will be a car waiting for you there. Good luck," Bosse said, standing.

Trueblood saluted him again. "I won't let you down, Sir."

"I know you won't. You're a Marine."

Chapter 75

I was led to the bedroom and cuffed to the headboard. The fight that I felt in my blood only moments ago had now gone. I felt defeated. All I had been working for the last five years came down to one conclusion. I had been feeding the man responsible for all the information I had gathered. I felt like a fool.

And now, I had even been tricked by the girl I thought I was falling in love with. Why was a woman like Jenny tied to a man like Buck?

I lay on the bed, thinking about all the bad things that had happened to me when I realized that what I should be thinking about was escape and survival.

I looked around the room, taking in all the pertinent details. The walls were bare but for the dingy squares around where pictures had once hung. There was a nightstand next to the bed. On it sat a single plastic bottle of water. A double light bulb ceiling fixture with glass shades, meant to resemble tulips, hung from the center of the room. One bulb was burned out, the other was probably a forty watt, I surmised by the dim glare it made on the green walls.

Other than that, the room was empty. The rugs had been removed, evident from the faded rectangles on the floor. The curtains were pulled shut and glimpses of blinds were faintly visible behind them.

My thoughts turned to how poorly the room was decorated. Buck had lived here for ten years and hadn't taken the time to fix the place up, then I came to my senses again. The room had been emptied for me. It was the perfect prison.

I pulled at my restraints only to verify what I had already concluded. They weren't going to budge.

Only one hand and one leg were cuffed. I could reach my water, and I could turn over in bed. Very nice, I thought, I wouldn't die of thirst or get bed sores.

Turning and looking at the metal headboard, I could see scratches in the finish on the other side. Someone else had been cuffed to the bed at one time or another. The bad part was that I had never heard of anyone claiming to be imprisoned here. That meant whoever had been here was most likely dead.

I heard the door rattle and open. Buck entered the room. He was dressed in blue jeans and a t-shirt. I realized it was the first time I had seen him in anything other than his uniform.

For the first time also I realized how muscular he was. His arms tugged at the seams in the t-shirt. The fabric stretched to the point where it seemed the blood flow would be cut off.

He didn't look like the comforting public official I knew. He looked like a prize-fighter you might have nightmares about meeting in a dark alley.

"Cam," he said, "are you comfortable?"

"No, as a matter of fact, I'm not. I would like a Wild Turkey and an M16."

"The Wild Turkey I will bring you shortly. The M16..."

"Okay, I'll take the Wild Turkey."

"I guess you are wondering why I have done what I have done. I know we will never be friends again, but I will miss you nevertheless," Buck said as if we were old friends parting due to other obligations.

"Willie, you are a sick son of a bitch. How could you kill all those innocent people just to take their boats and sell them?"

"It was a perfect opportunity. Bill and Susan, with the help of John Trapper, already had the scam set up. I stumbled upon it while investigating a boat theft. I cut myself in, and the rest is history."

"Were they killing before you came along?"

"No, that was my idea. It helped me get in the mood for the big strike," Buck said with a childlike edge to his voice, almost giddy.

"Quantico?" I said.

"Yes, at first, but when I read about the president being in Miami Beach this week, I changed my plan. I will get the Marines at Quantico next time."

"You're going to assassinate the president?"

"Yeah, I thought I would."

"Does Jenny know this?"

"Cam, you're such a softy. Face it, Jenny is a bad person. She doesn't care who is getting killed as long as she gets paid. Who do you think killed your partner, Jack?"

322

"Jenny killed Jack?"

"Yes she did and then she killed Ronnie Pierce a moment later. She threw them both over the side of her boat, tied to concrete blocks. A woman who would do that has a hard heart, don't you think?"

"Yeah, I guess she does. But so do you."

"I didn't always, but first the Marine Corps taught me to kill from a distance so I wouldn't become involved with the targets. Then they killed the woman I loved so I wouldn't become attached to any of the common people in Iraq. Then, when I realized they were the ones who'd done it, they turned the blame on me. I hate the Marine Corps. Now I have the chance to kill the Commander and Chief. I have to do it. It's like karma."

"How are you going to kill the Marines responsible for your girlfriend's death if you die killing the president?"

"I changed my mind about dying this time. Amar will be sacrificed for the president."

"But if Amar is in this to revenge his daughter, why would he die now before the ones responsible are punished?"

"I didn't tell him. I do feel bad about that, but I will have his revenge for him."

"So what will you do?"

"I'm going to retire a hero in Iraq with a lot of money."

"Will Jenny die in your little plan?"

"You ask too many questions. None of this really concerns you," Buck said, changing his tone from conversational to confrontational.

"One more thing before you go," I said.

"Sure, what is it?"

"Did you kill Malinda?"

"No, I swear to you on my mother's grave I did not have anything to do with that. I never did find who killed her other than the drug cartel from Mexico. When her boat was found in the Bahamas, I traced it to a drug delivery from Playa Del Carmen."

Strangely, I believed him.

~*~

Buck said, "Let's go, Jenny. We need to go to your house and get anything you will want to keep, then to my office for my records."

"Give me a minute," she said. "I need to use the restroom."

Jenny went into the bathroom and locked the door. She took her cell phone from her pocket and texted Sanchez, telling him of the latest development.

Chapter 76

Amar and Kasim woke at the first beam of light that entered through the dusty warehouse windows.

They folded the blankets they had spent the night lying on the cold warehouse floor. Their suits were hung on a makeshift clothesline of electrical wire, strung from the van door to a metal stanchion. Before dressing, they both went to a nearby wall and relieved themselves.

"Are you ready? Today is going to be a big day," Amar said.

"Yes. Eight years I have been ready," Kasim said.

The two men stepped over the dead bodies blocking the door and opened it just far enough to squeeze out.

It was a warm day already, and the sun felt good on bones chilled from having slept on the concrete floor.

Amar turned his face to the sun and took in a big breath through his nostrils. "This is one thing I will miss," he said. "The comfort of the sun on my skin."

"Allah will provide the sun for you, my friend. He will fulfill any desire you wish."

"Yes, I must have faith."

They walked two blocks, turned right and walked two more. There they entered a café which had a sign in front on the walk that read, in big red letters, "Buffet Breakfast."

As they entered, Kasim picked up a newspaper from the counter and tucked it under his arm. They took a seat next to the window where they could see the activity on the street.

Cindy Moss, a very attractive sixty-something woman, came to their table. "What would you gentlemen like to drink?"

"Orange juice and coffee for me thank you," Amar said.

Kasim didn't answer. He was busy reading the front page of the newspaper.

"And for you, sir?"

Kasim glanced up and said, "Coffee," then quickly turned back to the paper.

"Are you gentlemen going to visit the buffet today?" Cindy asked.

"Yes, Ma'am" Amar answered.

"Okay, just help yourselves, and I'll get your drinks."

"Thank you," Amar said while Kasim kept his nose buried in the newspaper.

Cindy was good at reading people, from her years of waiting tables. She had put two children through school and college by bringing people bacon and eggs, steak and potatoes and a smile.

Her husband had died in a car accident fifteen years before, and she had been left with the full financial burden. It had paid off when her son graduated from law school. He made sure she didn't want for anything, but she still enjoyed waiting on tables. She met some fascinating people.

These two, she surmised immediately, were not car salesmen. Maybe just as bad, though, probably terrorist she thought, stereotyping the two men.

She always liked to make up something about her customers. It was a game she enjoyed.

When the waitress left the table, Kasim said, "Look at this," and turned the paper for Amar to see.

On the front page, in big bold letters, it said, "PRESIDENT PAYTON TO VISIT MIAMI TODAY."

Under that, it told that he and his family would be cruising in on their yacht today and that he would be playing golf at the Miami Golf Club tomorrow. The article went on to tell of other family activities scheduled for the first family, but Amar quit reading.

"How are we going to be able to get to the marina today. We can't just drive in there with a bomb and load it on our boat," Amar said.

"What time will they be closing the docks?"

"He is scheduled to arrive at two o'clock. Probably before noon I would say."

"We must go now," Kasim said.

The two men got up and raced out of the café. They turned and ran down the street, back the way they had come.

Cindy watched them go then walked to the table and looked down at the paper. The headlines stared back at her, and an alarm went off in her head.

She went to her locker and retrieved her cell phone. She called the Miami FBI office.

Sanchez hung up his phone and called Agent

Wootton. "I'm down at the docks off of Little West River," he said. "I just got a call from the home office. A waitress reported two Iraqi men at her café a few minutes ago who came in for breakfast but ran out when they saw the headlines in the morning paper."

"About the President coming?" Wootton asked.

"Yeah, she thinks so. The café is only four blocks from here. I'm going to go over there. I'll keep a lookout for them. Where are you?"

"I'm on the way. I'll be there in ten minutes."

"Good. It's a long shot, but it's a shot."

Chapter 77

I was left alone in the room. I tugged at my restraints knowing full well I had no chance of freeing myself but still feeling the need to try.

Visions of animals gnawing off their tails or feet to free themselves from traps came to mind.

I didn't think I could stand the pain. Besides, I would have had to gnaw off one hand and a foot.

I turned my body, so I had one foot on the floor. As quietly as possible, I dragged the bed toward the window. It only moved an inch at a time and made a terrible scraping sound when it did.

I could now reach the window. I pulled back the curtain and exposed the blinds which I eased open by spreading two of the slats. My heart sank when I saw that behind them was a boarded-up window. That's when Billie Daryl walked into the room.

"Hey, Cam, can I help you with that," he said and laughed.

I collapsed back down onto the bed.

He made no attempt to move me away from the window or punish me for trying to escape.

"I'm supposed to check on you once in a while. Do you need anything?"

"No thanks, I'm just fine," I said sarcastically.

"Okay, see ya," and he turned to leave.

"Wait," I said. "Buck said he was going to get me a Wild Turkey."

Billie Daryl looked at me for a minute and then smiled.

"One Wild Turkey coming up."

With that, he left the room.

I knew I wouldn't be seeing him again for a long while so I continued to move the bed around the room. I reached the door and put my hand on the knob but felt it turn on its own.

It swung open, and Billie Daryl entered with my Wild Turkey in his hand. He flinched and looked up at me when he saw me standing so close. Out of reflex, I swung my right fist at him as hard as I could. I caught him on the jaw and felt it give. The Wild Turkey crashed to the floor and then so did Billie Daryl.

He fell outward, away from the door, but he didn't move. He was out cold.

I pulled the bed closer to the doorway and tried to reach him, but he had fallen further than I could stretch my cuffed arm.

I pulled at the bed even harder. What if he had the key in his pocket? Maybe they'd left it with him just in case I needed to go to the bathroom, or if they needed him to bring me to them somewhere.

The bed was pretty well jammed in the doorway and wasn't going any further.

I reversed my stance and reached out with my free leg. I could touch him with my foot.

I reached down, removed my shoe and sock and stretched my leg out to him again. I was able to get my toes under his belt and tugged at him. He moved slightly toward me, and I kept pulling until he was finally close enough that I could grab him with my free hand.

I pulled him through the doorway and searched his pockets. Bingo. The key was in his right pants pocket.

I tried it on the cuffs, and they sprang open. I put my shoe and sock back on and cuffed Billie Daryl to the bed, just like I had been.

I peeked out the bedroom door, half expecting to see a gun pointed at me. No one was there. I guessed if someone else were here, they would have heard all the racket. I walked through the living room and looked out the front window. There were no cars in the drive. I looked out the side window and saw Jenny's under the carport.

She must have left with Buck. If I left by the front door, I might be seen walking down the street.

I went to the back door and out into the pool area. Bucks forty-two foot Sea Ray was sitting at his dock. I climbed aboard and checked the ignition for the keys. They weren't there, so I checked under the Captains cushion. There they were. Very predictable.

I figured I could take the boat and cruise the canal until I hit open water and then ditch it at the first empty dock I saw. I started one engine and let it idle while I untied the lines. I pushed off and aimed the boat down the canal, a free man once more, in more than one sense of the term. Now I had time to think about Jenny. Even knowing what I then knew, I didn't want anything bad to happen to her. That was except for a long prison term for the murder of Jack. Ronnie's murder could be forgiven.

I didn't have to go far. I passed under the bridge at Cross Street and pulled the boat into an empty dock. It didn't look like anyone was around and the dock wasn't visible from the street. It might take Buck a while to find his boat.

I walked along the canal until I could get to Hurricane Hole without being seen. The bartender let me use the phone and I called Stacy.

Chapter 78

Agent Wootton arrived in the West Little River easternmost area ten minutes after talking to Sanchez.

Communicating by radio, they did their best to set up a search grid. They called the local police department for assistance. Together they had the area covered but knew it would take a lot of luck to find two Iraqi men in this mostly Hispanic neighborhood.

Amar stood at the window of the warehouse and

watched a black SUV with blue flashing lights speed past the building.

"Something has tipped them off," he said to Kasim.

"Maybe they are not looking for us."

"Maybe, but we cannot take the chance. We have to get the van out of here and to the Marina before noon."

They dragged the now rigid bodies away from the door and opened it. Kasim drove the van out of the building, and Amar jumped in.

"I will stay out of sight. If they are looking for us they probably know that there are two of us," Amar said.

Kasim drove slowly, so as not to draw unwanted attention to the van. He turned onto Little River Drive and followed it toward Highway 95.

A city police car passed them heading west. Kasim watched it in the rearview mirror. Suddenly, the police cruiser's brake lights came on, and the car spun a 180 degrees turn.

"They saw us," Kasim said.

"Let's go," Amar shouted as he pulled his machine gun from the bag. He checked his clips and shoved a new one in.

Kasim floored the van and sped toward the highway. He took the highway entrance on two wheels and fought to keep the van upright.

Checking his rearview mirror again, he saw the cruiser closing in.

Amar broke the back window out of the van with the butt of the rifle. He pointed the barrel out and squeezed the trigger. The cruiser swerved and spun in a circle.

Kasim sped along the highway. He took the next exit and slowed as he entered another neighborhood.

As he crossed through an intersection, a black SUV came from his right side and clipped the rear end of the van.

The van spun halfway around and Kasim floored it again, jumped the curb and swerved back out on the side street.

The SUV followed only three feet off their bumper. Amar regained his kneeling position and fired another blast of bullets toward the SUV.

Agent Wootton ducked down in the seat and tried to keep the SUV on a straight track.

Another volley of gunfire and Wootton was forced to step on the brake. The SUV came to a halt.

The van sped away and turned right one block later.

Agent Sanchez raced toward the last position that Wootton had called in.

Amar could hear another noise he recognized as a helicopter. This wasn't good. Kasim looked out the window and up to the sky.

"They are right above us," he yelled to Amar.

"Keep going. We can't let them catch us."

Kasim was flying down side streets now, catching air when he bumped through intersections.

Sanchez saw the van coming straight at him. He hit the brakes and cut the wheel to turn the SUV sideways in the middle of the road, blocking its passage.

Kasim did the same. Both vehicles came to a halt in the middle of the road.

~*~

Agent Wootton stopped his SUV a half-block behind the van. Three squad cars pulled up behind him, and their officers got out and trained their weapons on the van.

Wootton held his hand up to them and shouted, "There might be a bomb in that van. Don't shoot."

The officers immediately dropped the aim of their weapons to the ground.

Two helicopters were now flying around in wide circles over the van and police. One was an FBI helicopter, the other was from the news channel.

This was a big story—whatever it was—the newsmen were sure. They went to live cam, and the cable stations broadcast the scene throughout the country.

Chapter 79

Sheriff Buck and Jenny returned to his house. When they entered, the TV was on.

Billie Daryl was nowhere to be seen in the living room, but the scene on the TV screen caught Buck's eye.

"Holy shit!" he yelled.

Jenny turned to look at the TV too.

"My God, is that what I think it is?"

"Yeah, it's Amar and Kasim. It looks like they didn't make it to the marina."

"What are we going to do now?"

Buck ignored her and kept watching the scene unfold. The talking head in the corner of the TV was saying something about a possible bomb in the van.

Buck could see Amar and Kasim through the powerful lens of the camera. They were sitting calmly and talking.

"What the hell are they going to do?" Buck said. "Are they going to surrender?"

Jenny walked to the bedroom to check on Cam. The sight she saw made her heart skip a beat. Billie Daryl was sleeping like a baby on the bed, his hand and leg cuffed to the posts.

"Way to go, Cam," she said to herself.

She returned to the living room. Buck was still glued to the TV

"Is there a danger of the bomb going off?" she asked him.

He turned and looked at her. "Would that bother you if it did?"

"I just don't want a lot of innocent people to get hurt."

"Sometimes innocent people have to suffer for the better of the masses," he said.

"Is there any way to disarm it?"

"Yeah, I can do it with my phone."

Jenny pulled her gun and pointed it at Buck's head. She pulled back the hammer. He heard it and turned toward her.

"What the hell, Jenny?"

"Disarm the bomb," she said.

"Why?"

She reached into her pocket and pulled out her FBI badge.

He looked at it for a second then back into her eyes and finally laughed.

He turned back to the screen.

"Come on, Amar, don't give in," he said to the TV.

Just then, the van sped forward. The camera showed Agent Sanchez diving out of the way at the last minute and the van sideswiping his SUV as it blew by.

"Ha!" Buck said. "Look at that."

"Didn't you hear what I just said, Buck? Disarm the damn bomb," Jenny repeated, pointing the gun at Buck's head again.

Buck reached into his pocket and pulled out a small .22 caliber pistol.

Jenny pulled the trigger. Nothing happened.

"I found your gun earlier when you were in the bathroom. I took the privilege of unloading it. Hope you don't mind."

Buck walked Jenny to the bedroom.

"Ah shit," he said. "Billie Daryl, you stupid son of a bitch."

"You mean Mike Garrison don't you?" Jenny said.

"Well, I guess you have it all figured out."

"Most of it. Enough to know you'll never get away with it."

"I'll get away with it."

"No, you won't. There's nowhere to go."

"My guess is that the part you don't know is that I changed my plan about taking the chance of blowing up Quantico. The president coming along was just a bonus. I found a good way to get rid of Amar and still get my revenge."

"Your revenge?"

"Yeah, you know, for killing Farah."

"You killed Farah."

"No, I didn't. That part you got wrong because Bosse and Trueblood made it look that way. They killed her."

"So what will you gain from killing the president?"

"After I do it, I will announce to the world that the reason the President died was because he was aiding and abetting criminals.
I will have my revenge for the only woman I ever loved, and I will be a hero in Iraq. Not to mention very rich."

"You're sick."

"Yeah, I know. I've been told."

"All of this for a woman?" Jenny said.

"Well, not all for a woman. Actually, most of it was for the six million dollars we raised through boat jacking, drug sales and donations from sympathizers who would also like to see an attack on the United States."

"So you did it for money."

"Finally, you figured it out."

Jenny sighed.

"Into the bedroom," Buck said.

He tossed Jenny the keys and told her to free Billy Daryl. She did, but he still didn't move.

"Get some water and wake him up," he said.

Jenny filled a glass with water from the bathroom and poured it over Billy Daryl's head. He snorted and then woke.

"Wha a hell," he said in a muffled voice.

Feeling his jaw, he said, "Ma Futing ja e bro."

"Don't talk. You sound stupid," Buck said to him. "Any idea where Cam went?"

Billie shook his head.

"Get up. We have to find him."

"Why do you need Cam? It's all over now," Jenny said.

"Nothing is over. I'm still going to take my six million and go to Iraq and live like a king."

"Then go," Jenny said.

"Nope. Not until Cam is dead."

"What about me? Are you going to kill me too?"

"Maybe, it depends."

"On what?"

"On if you'll help me get out of the country."

"I might. What's in it for me?"

"You get to live, and I'll give you two hundred thousand."

"What about Billie Daryl? You going to kill him?"

Billy Daryl looked intensely at Buck.

"Of course not. He'll get two hundred thousand, and he can go live where-ever he wants."

Billie Daryl smiled at this.

"But first we have to find Cam. He knows too much. He'll have me caught before I even get to the airport."

Chapter 80

The van tore down the street at breakneck speed, back toward Highway 95.

Wootton and Sanchez ran back to their vehicles and jumped in. The van had a good lead, but Sanchez knew there were other cruisers on their way.

Kasim took the on-ramp and sped toward Highway 95. It would only take minutes, and then he would be at the Miami Golf Club minutes after that.

"What are we going to do when we get to the golf club?" Kasim asked.

"We'll drive the van into the clubhouse and then run on foot in all the commotion. We can detonate the bomb from our cell phone later," Amar said.

The van was only about two minutes from the golf club when it was struck by another police car, on the left rear bumper. The van spun around twice, hit the guard rail and flipped onto its side. The bomb did not explode.

Buck was watching all the action on TV again.

"Crap, it looks like it's over this time," he said.

"Good," Jenny said.

They watched as the van was surrounded by police and FBI vehicles. Two officers ran to the van and pulled Amar out. They leaned him against the van and one returned to get Kasim.

Buck pulled his cell phone out of his pocket and dialed a number. "This is how you disarm a bomb," he told Jenny and hit the send button.

Jenny watched as the van blew up. The nearby cars and personnel just disappeared in a white flash. The helicopter filming the scene started to spin and crashed to the ground.

"No," Jenny yelled.

"That bomb just destroyed everything in a half-mile radius. I hope none of those men were your friends," he said to Jenny.

"YOU SON OF A BITCH," she yelled and attacked Buck.

He hit her with one big fist, and she went down and out.

"Load her into the car," he told Billie Daryl. "We'll go find Cam and then get rid of both of them."

Buck went to the back door and looked out at his dock. "Son of a bitch stole my boat. I guess we'll have to use Jenny's."

I was in Stacy's houseboat. I didn't know if Buck would think to look here or not. If we would have had the TV on, we would have known a lot more than we did now, but unfortunately, we didn't want the distraction.

"Are you going to call the police?" Stacy asked.

"No, not yet. For one thing, I don't know which ones, if any, are working with Buck."

I looked out the window and up and down the dock. "This is crazy," I said, "I can't keep looking over my shoulder forever."

Stacy brought me a drink. "Wild Turkey on the rocks, right?" she said, holding the glass up to me.

"Perfect," I said.

I took the drink and downed it.

"Another?" she asked.

"No. I better not. I need to think clearly."

"Do you think Buck would have killed you?"

"Yeah, I think he would have. I think he would kill anyone who gets in the way of his goal, whatever that really is. It didn't all add up when he was telling me how he wanted justice for his girlfriend. That was eight years ago. He could seek out the man who he says killed her and shoot him. He was a sniper. I know he could hit his target."

"Cam, I'm not exactly worldly, but I do know that only a few things motivate men. Sex, money, power and revenge," she counted on her fingers. "I don't see any sex in this scenario, and if you don't think its revenge, then that leaves money and power. Sometimes the two are one."

"You're right. There is a lot of money involved in this, and the money would give him power. The power would bring an unlimited amount of sex and sex would, maybe in his mind, exact revenge. Kind of like, they can slow me down for a while, but they can't stop me," I said.

"Makes sense to me, but that doesn't really help us, does it?"

"No, it doesn't. It might help us to understand him a little, though."

Stacy's cell phone rang. She looked at the caller ID but didn't recognize the number. She answered anyway.

"Hello."

"Stacy, this is Sheriff Buck. May I talk to Cam please?"

Stacy's eyes grew large, and she looked at me and mouthed "Buck."

I shook my head.

"Cam isn't here," she said.

"I believe he is."

"I haven't seen him."

"I tell you what. Just for kicks, put your phone on speaker and lay it down. That way if Cam should walk in during my conversation he will have the option of picking up."

Stacy did as Buck asked. She shrugged at me.

"Hello, Cam. Can you hear me?"

I said nothing.

"Very well," he continued, "I thought you might want to know that I have Jenny with me. Why would that concern you, you might ask? Well, I just found out that Jenny is with the FBI. Imagine my surprise. By the way, did you see the explosive news today?"

I motioned for Stacy to turn on the TV. The screen lit up with major chaos. Ambulances and police cars were everywhere, and the remains of cars and a helicopter were on one side of a split-screen.

"What the hell did you do?" I yelled.

"Cam, I guess you just walked in. If you want to see Jenny alive again, I need you to meet me. I want to make sure the two of you aren't going to turn me over to the police before I can get out of the country. You'll be free to go once I'm gone."

"How do I know Jenny is with the FBI?"

"First of all her name isn't Jenny. It's Robin Anderson. Sweet girl. It would be a shame."

I thought about all the times when I'd doubted Jenny or Robin. It made sense she was with the FBI. That would explain a lot.

"Don't hurt her. Where do you want to meet?"

"First of all, no cops. If I see one just driving by, I'll kill her."

"Don't worry," I said.

"Next, bring Stacy with you."

"No."

"Yes!" he demanded.

"No. I'll make sure she doesn't talk, but you're not going to get her."

There was a pause on the other end of the phone. I could tell he didn't like to lose, but he was running out of time.

"We'll bring Jenny's boat to your dock in one hour."

"I'll be here."

The line was disconnected.

"Okay, Stacy, it's time for you to get out of here. When is Barbie supposed to get back?"

"Not for a few days yet."

"Pack a bag quickly. Go to Marathon and stay with Barbie. I'll call you when it's safe for you to return."

Stacy didn't argue. She had her bag packed in five minutes and was ready to go.

"Be careful, Cam. Are you sure there isn't something I can do to help?"

"No. I'm good," I said.

Stacy put her arms around me and kissed me softly on the lips.

"Please be here when I get back," she said, looking into my eyes.

"I plan to be," I choked out.

Stacy smiled, "You're so cute."

Chapter 81

I had an hour to kill. That was exactly what I'd wanted to do—kill. I used the time to walk around my boat. It was still a wreck. Nothing had been done to it in the last few days. I stepped on board and poked around in the rubbish for some kind of a weapon. All I found was a big piece of angle iron but had no idea where it might have come from.

I stepped back out and was greeted by Billie Daryl. He was pointing a gun at me and didn't look too happy.

"I shu jus shoo ya," he said.

"What?"

"I shu jus shoo ya."

I looked at him with a puzzled expression.

"Shu ya," he said. **"I shu shoo ya."**

I knew what he'd said the first time but couldn't help myself.

"Oh, I get it," I said. "Hey, I'm sorry for hitting you, but you scared me. It was just a reflex."

"Fa ya," he said.

"Why are you here?"

"Th wah ya."

"To watch me?"

"Yah."

"Would you like a drink?"

He looked at me, and I could tell he was thinking about it.

"Wild Turkey," I said.

"O hay,"

I took that for an okay.

"Follow me."

We walked back down to Stacy's boat and retrieved the bottle and a couple of glasses from the table.

"I really felt bad about hitting you," I said as I poured his drink.

I poured one for myself too. I turned and handed him his and then held mine up for a toast.

"Forgive me?"

He clinked glasses with me and took a drink. That was when I hit him again. He went down even harder this time. He would really be mad, but it would be a week or so now before he could even think about coming after me.

I retrieved his gun and stuck it in the back of my pants. At least I was armed now.

I checked his pockets and found a cell phone. I dialed Diane's number. Still no answer. I was really starting to worry about her.

I heard a boat coming. I wrestled Billie Daryl inside Stacy's boat and closed the door. I went back to my own and waited.

Jenny's forty-two foot Baha came into sight. Buck was driving, and Jenny was lying on the seat. I let the boat bump the dock and then grabbed the line and tied it off.

"Where's Billie Daryl?" Buck said.

"Haven't seen him."

"That damn idiot."

"What's wrong with Jenny?" I asked.

"She's okay. I was just about to wake her."

Buck opened a plastic bottle of water and poured it on Jenny's head.

She moved a little and then opened her eyes. She put her hand on her chin.

"You bastard," she said. "You murderer."

"Okay, we've already been over all that. Now I just want to put that behind us and be friends," Buck said.

Jenny, or Robin I guess, gave Buck the finger.

He turned to me. "Women, can't live with them…"

'What's your plan?" I asked.

"Go get Billie Daryl," Buck said.

"He's not here."

"Yes, he is. I told him to be here, so he's here. If you don't get him now, I'll put a bullet in your girlfriend's leg. Then we can both watch her bleed out."

I walked back to Stacy's boat, dragged Billie Daryl out from under the table and threw him over my shoulder. I walked back to Jenny's boat, stepped up to the platform and dropped him on the floor.

"Idiot," Buck said.

"He's going to be mad, isn't he?" I said.

"No, we're going to go drop him off where we dropped the others," Buck said.

"The others?"

"Let's go, Jenny. You're driving."

"Now way," Jenny said.

"Okay," Buck said, "here's how this is going to work. If Jenny doesn't do what I say, I'll shoot

Cam. If Cam doesn't do what I say, I'll shoot Jenny. And really, I want to shoot somebody."

Jenny got behind the wheel, and I untied the lines. She backed us out and turned toward the open water.

"Where to?" she said.

"You know the spot. Go to where you dropped off Jack and Ronnie," Buck said and laughed.

Jenny turned on the GPS and guided the boat north along the coast and then steered north-east.

Another boat shadowed them from a mile back. It was just dark enough now that if the boat ran without lights, it would not be seen.

Jenny slowed the boat and said, "We're here. Are you planning to kill us now?"

"My plan is to drop Billie Daryl off," he said. "Cam, you haven't got to do this yet. Tie that block to Billie's ankle."

I hesitated, and he turned the gun toward Jenny.

"Okay, I'll do it."

Jenny stopped the boat and flipped some switches. The boat made a low humming noise.

"What's that?" Buck asked.

"Pumps," Jenny said. "I have to pump it every time I stop."

"Have you got that block on yet?" Buck asked me.

"Yes, but why don't you just let him go? He can't turn you in."

"Sit him up on the edge of the boat," he said.

I did. I felt very bad but knew if I didn't do it, he would shoot Jenny, and then make me do it anyway.

While I was lifting him to the rail, I took the opportunity to slip my gun from the back of my pants.

Buck grabbed my wrist and slapped on a handcuff. He then slapped the other cuff to Billie Daryl's wrist.

He forced the gun from my hand and threw it over the side of the boat.

"If you find that gun down there, you can use it to kill yourself," he said and laughed wildly.

I knew this was probably my last few seconds on earth. I turned to Jenny and said, "I love you."

"I love you too, Cam," she said.

"Oh, you guys are choking me up," Buck said. "Just think, Cam, you're only twenty feet from Malinda, and all you can say is that you love another woman."

"You bastard, you did kill her."

"I didn't want too, but I had no choice. Tell her I'm sorry,"

He stepped toward me to push me over. Just then, Billie Daryl jumped. A big hole opened up in his head.

Just as we realized he had been shot, another shot hit the boat. Buck ducked down, and Jenny ran toward me. I thought she was going to pull me to safety, but instead, she pushed Billie Daryl and me over the side of the boat.

Buck ran toward the cabin. He didn't make it. A bullet caught him in the neck, and he went down.

Jenny dove over the other side of the boat, swam around to the back and looked to see where the shots might have come from. The darkness was doing a fine job of protecting the shooter. She waited until she heard a boat start in the distance and the sound of the motor moving farther away.

Ted Trueblood had done his job. He hoped he had not hit the girl. Commander Bosse would be happy to know that their secret would now be safe.

Jenny swam around to the other side of the boat where she had pushed Cam. "CAM, ARE YOU ALRIGHT?" she yelled.

I was lying in a net with Billie Daryl on top of me. I pushed him off and stuck my head back up to take a much- needed breath.

"CAM," Jenny yelled again.

"JENNY," I yelled back.

"STAND UP," she said.

I did, and put my hand on the side of the boat for balance. I couldn't believe it, a net with a metal frame had slid out from the hull. That was what the sound had been when she'd stopped.

Jenny swam to the net and climbed in. She put her arms around me and kissed me. "Did you say you loved me?"

"That was before you pushed me into the ocean with a concrete block and a dead guy."

"It was only *Knee Deep*," she said and kissed me again.

Epilogue

We radioed in our position to the Miami FBI office. They sent a helicopter to pick up Robin, Buck, Billie Daryl and me. They dropped off an agent who would take the boat back to the docks for us.

It was a short flight and car ride to the FBI offices. Robin held my hand the whole way.

As we entered the building, Diane ran to me and threw her arms around me. I hugged her equally as hard. I had been afraid I would never see her again, and couldn't stand the thought.

Robin hugged Diane and excused herself. "I'll see you inside in a few minutes," she said.

"Cam, are you okay?" Diane asked, looking me over for any wounds I might have gotten.

"Couldn't be better," I said. "How about you?"

"Why would you care?"

"Because I've discovered that if there is one person in my life I can't live without, it's you."

Diane kissed me on the cheek.

I stepped back and looked at her. She stared into my eyes, and I could feel my heart melting.

I thought about what Robin had said. Did Diane really have a thing for me?

"I'm so relieved to see you're alright," I said. "We had better get inside."

Diane kissed me on the cheek again, took my hand and walked through the doors with me.

Jenny or that is Robin, was waiting for us in a debriefing room. I walked in and saw that the room was filled with at least seven other agents. There were TV screens on the wall, and they were all showing different scenes of the bombing.

"That was awful," I said.

"It could have been worse," a voice from behind me said.

I turned to see Jack standing there.

"Jack," I said excitedly, "I thought you were dead."

"No, are you kidding? That net caught me just when I thought I was a goner. Robin wouldn't let anything happen to us."

No, I guess she wouldn't, even if I did cuss her and give her the finger. She was our protector.

"What about Ronnie Pierce?" I asked.

"She arrested him for attempted murder as soon as he pushed me over the side. Then he spilled his guts, which helped them get closer to Buck."

I couldn't believe it. It had been a hell of a ride. Two hours ago I thought I had lost everything and was going to die myself, but now I have it all.

Robin joined the three of us. "We need to go over a few details and then you guys are free to go. We can get the rest tomorrow."

Half an hour later, we were finished for the night.

"See you tomorrow around eleven. Okay?" Robin said.

"Sounds good," I said.

"Cam, I don't know what your intentions are," Jack said, "but if you're not going to ask Robin out, I would like to invite her to dinner tomorrow."

Diane took Jack's hand. "Come on, big boy, you're out of your league this time. That one is taken."

Jack feigned disappointment. "I knew I should have moved faster."

"Robin, can you take Cam to your place tonight? I think I'll drop this one off and go home for a good night's rest," Diane said.

"I think I could find a spot on the couch for him," she said.

Diane kissed me again, this time on the lips. She turned to Jack and took his hand. "You know I'm not doing anything tomorrow for dinner," she said to him.

Jack looked at me. I said, "Don't even think about it."

"You don't trust me with your daughter?" he said.

"No."

"Sorry, Diane," he said.

"You can't watch me forever you know," she said, smiling an extra sexy smile at me.

Jack looked at me again.

"No," I repeated.

~*~

Robin took me to her house. We opened a bottle of wine and sat on the back patio.

"What are we going to do now?" I asked.

"I've got a good idea," she said, taking my hand.

"I mean after that. What about us. What's *our* next step?"

"Well, I think your next step is to go back to New York and finish your internship with Chad. I worked hard to get that set up with the Bar Examiner."

"You did that?"

"I needed to get you out of the way, but you just wouldn't stay gone."

"I'll be in New York, and you'll be in Miami," I said, "that's not going to work."

"Oh, didn't I tell you? There is an opening in the New York FBI office. I got it, and a promotion. They thought I handled this case so well they agreed to anything I wanted."

"In that case," I said, taking her hand and pulling her to her feet, "I have a case that needs some handling."

The End

Other Books by Mac Fortner:

<u>Sunny Ray Series</u>:

Rum City Bar

Battle for Rumora

<u>Cam Derringer series</u>:

<u>Knee Deep</u>

Bloodshot

Key West: Two Birds One Stone

Murder Fest Key West

Coming in October 2019:

Hemingway's Treasure

About Mac Fortner

Mac grew up in Evansville, Indiana, where he attended high school and college. He lived in The Philippine Islands and Viet Nam for two and a half years while serving his country as a helicopter crew chief.

He has written many songs over the years. All his songs are short stories, so he decided to convert them to novels, adding suspense and humor to the plots.

These books can be found at
www.macofortner.com
Or
On Amazon

MAC FORTNER